WAKING DREAM?

Desperately, Vair reached for the energy staff, trying to tug it loose from the straps that held it in place across O'Neill's back. O'Neill pushed the alien away, and in their struggle the staff came free and drifted down to the sandy sea floor. Vair dived after it, and O'Neill kicked hard to get there first. As he claimed the weapon, Vair took his hand, and pointed.

Not ten meters away, one of the octopi had a small coral-creature in his tentacles, and the massive beak was poised to crunch through its skull.

O'Neill had a solid conviction that anybody who was trying to kill a kid was by definition not a good guy. He raised the energy staff and fired.

The bolt of energy flashed, sizzled, and dissipated in the water.

For some reason, the staff wouldn't work. He reached for the zat gun, and got the same result. The weapo   were   it was the water,   some other reaso   pped the gun, an   vhich was still f   beak open, as if waiting for a cue to

The next moment man and alien were standing in the middle of the desert, as dry as if they'd never been near a body of water in their lives. . . .

THE MORPHEUS FACTOR

A Stargate SG - 1™ Novel

Ashley McConnell

Based on the story and characters created by
Dean Devlin & Roland Emmerich

Developed for Television by
Jonathan Glassner & Brad Wright

A ROC BOOK

ROC
Published by New American Library, a division of
Penguin Putnam Inc., 375 Hudson Street,
New York, New York 10014, U.S.A.
Penguin Books Ltd, 27 Wrights Lane,
London W8 5TZ, England
Penguin Books Australia Ltd,
Ringwood, Victoria, Australia
Penguin Books Canada Ltd, 10 Alcorn Avenue,
Toronto, Ontario, Canada M4V 3B2
Penguin Books (N.Z.) Ltd, 182–190 Wairau Road,
Auckland 10, New Zealand

Penguin Books Ltd, Registered Offices:
Harmondsworth, Middlesex, England

First published by Roc, an imprint of New American Library,
a division of Penguin Putnam Inc.

First Printing, February 2001
10 9 8 7 6 5 4 3 2 1

CHAPTER ONE

"If it's Tuesday, it must be P4V-837," Jack O'Neill announced as SG-l stepped through the gate. He sniffed at the air and then took a deep, appreciative breath. "Temperature balmy, flowers in bloom, skies blue, gravity norm— *Hey!*"

Across a lovely meadow, a massive cottonwood tree heaved itself free of the earth and shook the dirt loose from ropy gray roots.

It wasn't really a cottonwood, of course. Aside from the fact that Terran cottonwoods were a little less animate, the "tree" was zebra striped. Nonetheless, the trunk's base color was gray, and the mass of heavy, twisted branches supported silvery-green leaves. As Daniel had once remarked in passing, the human mind sought to put all new experiences into a known context, at least initially. And it *looked* like a cottonwood. A *walking* cottonwood.

"What the—"

The four members of SG-1 stood at the foot of the little hill that marked the Stargate on this world and stared as the tree's branches rattled against each other, the leaves making a swishing sound.

A shadow passed between the team and the sun, chilling them to the bone, and Daniel Jackson looked up.

"Uh, Jack. That's a roc, Jack. That's a really, really, *really* big roc."

"That's a bird." Samantha Carter gripped her automatic rifle tensely, watching as the shadow flapped its wings with the sound of thunder. It wheeled above them and swooped down to snatch up the cottonwood in one impossibly huge claw. The sixty-foot tree was the size of a twig in the creature's foot. The roots and branches beat futilely at the massive legs.

"No, it's definitely a roc," Daniel assured her.

"I thought that was something out of mythology," O'Neill said nervously, looking around for the DHD while at the same time keeping an eye on the tree thrashing frantically in the clutches of a bird the size of a small mountain. The bird had a massive, curved beak and brilliant green feathers that could be used to roof houses. It also had very impressive claws that wrapped around the gnarled trunk of the tree in a very efficient manner.

"It is," Daniel agreed. "Arabian mythology. Second voyage of Sinbad. Enemy of giant snakes."

"Then what is it doing here?" Teal'C asked as the bird launched itself back into the sky. "And how can it fly? The wingspan cannot support it."

The team had fallen back to the DHD, just in case the giant bird looked their way. Fortunately, it seemed to be fully occupied by its prey, if a tall vegetable could be called prey. Three or four more giant birds appeared, standing by if the first should happen to drop the thing.

"Ask a bumblebee," Jack said. Behind them, the Gate closed.

The next tree over began to shrug back and forth, tugging its roots free from the bank of earth by the stream. It wasn't clear whether the second tree was planning on going to the aid of the first or not. Meanwhile, the roc was gaining altitude, and its friends continued to hover. One or two were attracted by the new movement and swooped at the new target.

"Was there *anything* in the M.A.L.P. data that mentioned this?" Carter asked plaintively.

"Uh, not that I saw," Daniel responded.

"It was not in my copy of the briefing report."

"Mine either," Carter said, "and I'd really like to know why!"

"Is it just me," O'Neill said, eyeing the overly active landscape, "or is that tree trying to chase us?"

"I don't know about the tree, Colonel, but those spiders are definitely heading our way."

"*Spiders!* What spiders!" Jackson yelped.

A wave of small, extremely aggressive brown arachnids swarmed out of the ground at their feet.

"I don't think those are technically spiders—" Carter offered, stepping hard on a dozen or so.

"I don't care! Get them *off* me!" Jackson said.

"Normally," O'Neill said, batting frantically at the waves of multilegged organisms tickling their way up his pants legs, "I'd say we have a duty to explore this planet, fulfill our mission, and report back. Under the circumstances—" he ducked away from an aggressive swipe by a branch six inches in diameter—"I suggest we let the machines gather more data . . ."

"Signal to open the iris already sent," Jackson reported, kicking at a tree root trying to get between him and the DHD. "Entering—"

And the tree root was gone.

The writhing wood Jackson had just bruised his foot on vanished. He wiggled his toes—yes, they still hurt like hell.

The bugs were gone too. O'Neill kept brushing at his clothing, as if not convinced, but they'd vanished.

The circling rocs overhead, the thrashing trees, the waves of almost spiders were all gone.

The four of them stood alone in a lovely meadow beside the DHD, not far from the Stargate. They spun in place, trying to see all around themselves and up in the sky at the same time.

A meadow. Tall, respectably stationary zebra-striped "cottonwoods" waving gently in the breeze. Soft spongy grayish-green grass underfoot dotted with little starlike purple-and-yellow flowers. Puffy white clouds high in the sky. The brooding stone circle of the Stargate, and the dome of the DHD with its panel of symbols.

Waves splashing on a beach that hadn't been there moments before.

The four of them. And that was all.

"Uh. Did anyone else see . . . could we have all hallucinated. . . ?"

"I do not believe it was a hallucination, Daniel Jackson." Teal'C was frowning at a welt on the back of one hand.

"Well, my toes don't think so either, but I guess I could have kicked the Dial-Home Device."

O'Neill shook his head, as if to get the remaining spiders out of his military-trimmed hair. "I don't remember seeing a large body of water reported," he stated, glaring ominously at a tangle of black-and-yellow kelp washing ashore. "And it wasn't here when we stepped through." He sniffed deeply. "It didn't smell like this a little while ago either." A gull—or at least something that looked remarkably *like* a gull— swooped by. It was a distinctly ordinary-size bird. O'Neill strode over to the kelp, splashing the shallow shifting water hard with his combat boots. It was real, as real as soaked socks could get. "Okay, folks, this is officially too weird. I think we'll just skip this one."

Daniel, still flexing his toes and feeling grateful for combat boots, objected. "Oh, come on, Jack. It's an alien world. It's *supposed* to be weird. We can't go running home to Hammond every time something unusual happens."

O'Neill paused in the middle of shifting his pack and stared at the other man. Daniel Jackson, a civilian, stared right back. The other two members of Stargate SG-1 glanced at each other uneasily, and Carter stepped back out of range of the glares.

As she did so, she nearly tripped. The action was enough to break the rising tension, to the relief of both participants.

"Hey," Carter muttered. "This looks manufactured." She reached down and picked up a small round pot and promptly dropped it again. "Ouch! That's hot!"

The team crowded around, and Jackson, the team anthropologist, went to one knee and picked up the artifact to examine it. He too put it back down and then wrapped a handkerchief around his hand to protect it. "Handmade," he said. He sniffed at it and promptly sneezed, waving away a tendril of smoke coming from a charred lump stuck to the bottom of the pot. "Whew. There're your flowers, Jack." He looked up at the others. "And that's why we should stick around. There are people on this world. And that's our mission, isn't it? 'To perform reconnaissance, determine threats, and if possible make peaceful contact.' We can't do that if we turn tail just because the landscape's a little bizarre."

O'Neill bit back an angry reply. Jackson was right, of course. But so was he. They had no business on a world where they couldn't trust their own senses.

However, just because he was morally certain a threat existed didn't mean he'd "determined" it yet. And he sure hadn't scoped out its potential either for or against the interests of Earth. Daniel was right: They needed to find out more before they retreated.

And he wasn't going to let the scientist get away with implying anything either. He looked down at the top of Daniel's head as the kneeling man inhaled the remaining scent of whatever had burned in the little pot. Maybe it was just a reflex on his part, O'Neill thought. Maybe it was just paranoia. But he still wanted to haul out of here.

Which was not the same thing at *all* as "turning tail."

"All right," he said at last. "We'll look around a little more. See if we can find out what's going on." *But I still don't like it,* he thought.

Perhaps they can help us.

They may help the others too.

Not if we seek them first.

Beyond aught else, they will have new dreams. Different dreams. Approach them. Make them welcome. We need their help, whether they will it or not.

Very well.

Elsewhere, four small, furry humanoids crouched in the middle of a circle of smudge pots, staring down at a miniature image of SG-1 that took up the small space in the center of the circle. One of the humanoids looked up. *Let us go to meet them then. We need them badly.*

Another sighed in acquiescence. *Go. I will remain and shape as I can.*

*   *   *

"I didn't think cottonwoods would grow around saltwater," Carter said doubtfully, eyeing the now benign trees.

"Well, they're probably not real cottonwoods."

"They might be, Jack, if the Goa'uld planted a human colony here and they brought cottonwood seeds with them."

O'Neill glared at Jackson. "No, really? The possibility never occurred to me."

"Perhaps these persons can explain," Teal'C suggested, stepping between what promised to grow into a real squabble.

The other three members of SG-1 turned hastily away from the lapping water to face what Teal'C had already seen.

The inhabitants of P4V-837—who also did not appear in the M.A.L.P. data—weren't quite human, though they did walk on two legs and have two arms and heads on top. Bilaterally symmetrical in all respects, they were clothed in something that shimmered and blurred in the sunlight, as if it couldn't quite decide what it wanted to be. As they watched, the material, if it was material, shifted and flowed over the aliens' bodies until it was a reasonable facsimile of the team's fatigues.

"Ooooh-kay," O'Neill muttered. "Teal'C, where did they come from?"

"I am not certain," the Jaffa said. "Possibly the same place as the roc. They appeared . . . suddenly."

"Then maybe they're not real either."

The aliens approached to within a few feet of the team and stopped.

All three of the newcomers had large brown eyes, but their faces were covered with patterns of hair in different colors, growing in weblike lines and curlicues of red, brown, and silver fur, respectively. It was difficult to read expressions since five or six eyebrows seemed to radiate from the corners of their lips.

"Hello?" Daniel said tentatively.

The three aliens looked at each other and then back at the team.

"Hello," they responded, in chorus.

Despite the repetition, the word was clearly more than an echo: It carried meaning to the speakers as well as those spoken to. The members of SG-1 all let go unconsciously held breaths. Once again, the aliens spoke English. It was *such* a convenience when it worked out that way. Or maybe there was something about the transition through the wormhole that—usually—enabled the team to understand and speak the language of the destination planet. They'd never managed to figure it out, but it was nice when it happened.

"Uh, hi. We come in peace?" Daniel, having elected himself spokesman, pressed his position. O'Neill stood back, content to let the scientist do his thing while he himself tried to figure out what had happened to the spiders, not to mention the rocs.

The patterns of hair rippled across the three faces. O'Neill was pretty sure that meant the aliens were laughing at them. "You carry weapons," Silver pointed out.

"You never know when a tree is going to try to eat you," O'Neill muttered.

More writhing hair. One of the three turned away to look at the cottonwoods, and they could see that the hair patterns extended over the back of the skull as well. The patches of bare skin were clearly visible—the hair was at most three-quarters of an inch long on Red, who had, comparatively speaking, the most luxurious mane of the three. Brown was the tallest, and the top of his furry Mohawk barely came to Carter's shoulder.

"We carry weapons to protect ourselves, not to attack peaceful people," Daniel continued gamely. "We'd like to be friends."

"We'd like to understand what just happened here," O'Neill added rather waspishly.

"What happened?" The three faced each other again, and O'Neill caught a low mutter among them. Lip reading would be impossible with these guys, he thought, and then brought himself up short. There was no reason to assume they were male, he reminded himself. They might all be Samantha Carters.

In which case it was probably a good thing they weren't all as well armed as Major Carter, who was keeping a solid grip on her rifle, ready to bring it to bear in an instant. Teal'C was somewhat more comfortable with the situation, the butt end of his energy staff firmly grounded on the soft grass.

Brown broke out of the huddle and faced them, his mouth stretching wide as if he were parodying a smile. "We wish you welcome," he—or she—said. "Wise ones are ready to protect themselves whenever necessary, but we are no threat to you. We too wish to be friends. We wish to learn from you. Please come and eat with us. We can sit and talk and learn from one another."

The three aliens turned and took a few steps away, then looked back expectantly.

The team looked to its leader.

Its leader thought about it and shrugged. While he'd rather the M.A.L.P. had a chance to get more information about this weird place, the machine couldn't ask questions. Why not find out from the inhabitants? They certainly didn't look threatening, and they carried nothing that looked like weapons. But that didn't mean a thing really. O'Neill glanced at his team, gathering their opinions.

The original probe sent through the Stargate to this planet had sent back to Earth visual data showing a meadow—sans beach—and trees that looked enough like their counterparts on Earth to lead the science team to suspect the flora might have had its origin there. If that was the case, this world was a very hospitable place for Earth species—definitely a keeper. And the possibility that there might have been previous contact with Earth practically demanded investigation. On the other hand, there hadn't been any sign of intelligent life on this world, especially not transplanted human beings.

Of course, that was before the current landlords, if that was what they were, showed up. They weren't human, but they were certainly intelligent.

Of course, there hadn't been any video of walking trees and giant parrots either. So the machine had overlooked quite a few things.

Daniel was already moving forward. Carter, more suspicious, followed, eyeing the aliens warily. Teal'C exchanged a glance with O'Neill.

Unanimous then.

SG-1 followed.

The aliens led them across the meadow and through the trees, skipping nimbly over the exposed roots. The team went more warily, expecting those roots to start wriggling, but they remained still and firmly embedded in the earth.

O'Neill took the opportunity to glance back to the Gate and as a result actually saw the ocean vanish, as a mirage approached too closely will vanish. It was replaced with more meadow, more grass, and more trees. O'Neill sniffed deeply, but couldn't detect a lingering aroma of salt and fish and kelp. The beach was gone as if it had never been. Only the Stargate and its Dial-Home Device still remained, unchanged and unchanging.

But the laces on O'Neill's boots were still wet. His fingers closed more tightly on the butt of his pistol. He tried to remember if there had been an odder world among the many he'd trod upon since the Stargate was reactivated. God knew there had been a lot of strange ones: being alien was part and parcel of being alien, after all. It wasn't in and of itself a reason to cancel a mission. But it did make his teeth itch.

It was a pleasant walk, or it would have been if his feet were drier. He hung back to watch Daniel, who was eagerly conversing with the three aliens, gesticulating, nodding, pushing his glasses back up on his nose when they slipped down. Carter and Teal'C had fanned out on either side of

O'Neill, neatly flanking their hosts. They were as prepared for hostile action as they could be, considering that there were only four of them and one of the four was oblivious to the possibility that the friendly little aliens might turn into human-eating monsters without any warning at all.

Although, O'Neill had to admit, they didn't give any indication of being monstrous. And he didn't have the particular hair-rising-on-the-back-of-his-neck reaction that he usually got when they were walking into a trap.

Nonetheless, his teeth itched.

The open areas between the trees got smaller and smaller as they went on, until they were mostly in the shade. The trees were no longer cottonwoods either; there were a few aspens, familiar to O'Neill from innumerable ski weekends in Colorado, and more "other" trees—ones he couldn't identify. He wasn't a botanist, and he didn't expect to be able to reel off the names of every plant he encountered, but more and more of the trees looked like they came from a world that featured people with odd patterns of hair on their heads. The branches, for instance, marched up the trunks in perfectly symmetrical rows, and the bark was bright yellow. It just didn't look like home anymore.

The itch that said *Get out of here* was back. He looked over his shoulder. The Stargate was a long way back, but he was certain that he could retrace their path. Even if he couldn't, the tracer left by the DHD would home them in, should it become necessary.

On the other hand, there *was* a mission to perform. His own personal preferences couldn't be allowed to overrule that. He sighed to himself, resolved to keep his wits firmly about him, and kept going.

Silver looked back at him and the others and waved them up closer as they stepped through an opening between two trees and stopped abruptly. The ground fell away from their feet as if it had been sheared off by a knife. But the grasses still grew soft and cushiony down the nearly vertical slope. The trees lined up at the top of the slope as if looking down at their counterparts that grew at its base.

"Come and eat with us," Silver said, repeating its—his?—earlier invitation.

"Uh, I don't think so," O'Neill said.

"We ought to accept hospitality when it's offered," Daniel pointed out.

O'Neill gave him a long look, and a faint tinge of red touched Daniel's fair complexion. Behind that look were a hundred reminders of other times and other places and other invitations. "Said the fly to the spider," the colonel remarked dryly. "This place is just . . . *weird*."

CHAPTER TWO

"We haven't been threatened so far," Carter pointed out. "By the inhabitants, at least," she added hastily as her superior officer's look was directed her way. "They seem to be friendly. And maybe we can find out why . . . those other things . . . happened."

O'Neill always thought that his curiosity bump was as big as the next guy's, and Carter somehow knew how to scratch it. He weighed the phenomenon of walking trees and changing landscapes against the pint-size furry aliens with morphing clothes and decided, cautiously, to let curiosity win out for the time being.

"Come and eat with us," Silver repeated. "We're glad to see you. We'll have a party."

"Uh, were you expecting us?" Daniel inquired, pushing his glasses up on the bridge of his nose. He hadn't sneezed again since that first time, O'Neill noted.

"Oh, no, oh, no, we always welcome strangers. Come down to our home and eat with us. Stay with us and talk. We always welcome strangers. Come."

Get a lot of strangers here, do you? O'Neill asked himself acerbically. He was pleased to see Jackson actually asking the question as they trooped along. The little red alien babbled something in response about "many strangers, not like you." *So probably not Goa'uld. Maybe.* "But we welcome you, welcome you."

Something about the invitation reminded him of an old myth involving a trip to Hell and eating pomegranate seeds. He'd have to ask Daniel, who probably had the reference at his fingertips, if he could ever manage to pry the young archaeologist from the joy of interacting with yet another alien culture. The invitation to eat, however, raised a definite alarm. Once before they'd been welcomed with open arms, and he had eaten a welcoming feast. The result had been incredibly accelerated aging, and it had taken quite an effort to reverse it. He had no intention of being eligible for Social Security more than twice in his life.

He wondered if they were expected to roll down the hill, but the three aliens led them off along the crest of the slope for another hundred feet, and there before them appeared a long stone stairway laid upon the grass, leading grandly downward. O'Neill could have sworn it hadn't been there fifteen seconds earlier.

Definitely weird.

He looked back, but the Gate was still there, a distant arch barely visible over the tops of the trees. At least it hadn't morphed into a pink elephant or something. Nice to know there was still a back door available.

He scuffed at the rough yellow surface of the step in a tentative fashion. The others waited behind him while the three aliens paused a few steps below and looked back up at their visitors inquiringly.

As commanding officer, it was his decision to make; but when he took a silent vote of the rest of his team, Teal'C only raised an eyebrow, Carter offered no opinion, and Jackson, of course, couldn't wait to get going.

The slabs of rock, solid under his feet, took his weight without sinking, and the steps were sufficiently wide and shallow that he didn't have to look for a railing to balance himself. Apparently the slope only looked steeper than it was. Or maybe it was just another one of those weird things.

He inhaled deeply, let the breath out, and followed the little furry people, keeping one hand close to his sidearm just in case.

Behind him, he could hear Carter counting steps under her breath as they followed the aliens down. She reached seventy-eight by the time they got to the bottom. The three little aliens trooped along gamely, scurrying ahead and then pausing to look back and wave them on. Soon they entered what could have passed for a hardwood forest on Earth, with trees that looked like oaks, with broad boles and spreading limbs. The ground, though, was as bare of undergrowth as he'd expect to find in a pine forest. It made walking easier, but for some reason he had to squint to keep track of the three aliens leading them on. Their brightly colored fur patterns blended with the light and shadows cast by the sun through the leaves.

Eventually, they came to a valley and a village of small conical huts. The huts were built out of some woven fabric and resembled tipis. The three aliens scurried in one to announce their arrival. The settlement resembled a Plains Indian village, minus the paintings on the fabric—and the campfires, drying racks, and horses picketed outside. The huts were arranged in roughly square patterns around a central open area, a pattern O'Neill was beginning to find very familiar from one world to the next. Jackson would probably say that it was a logical pattern for herding societies or that most social species had typical centralized gathering places. In any case, it echoed patterns they'd seen before, and that was reassuring somehow. The place was weird, but not *that* weird.

He was relieved to find that, despite what the welcoming party had told them, no one was expecting them, and there wasn't a banquet laid out ready for interstellar guests. From out of the conical huts came dozens of people who were just as surprised to see visitors as their visitors were to see them. Brown, Red, and Silver did a lot of talking in that low, muttery whisper before the other aliens were convinced that the newcomers were staying awhile and started pulling dinner together. Small domesticated animals flopped, squawked, and scurried between the houses.

"Well, Daniel, what can you tell us?" O'Neill asked, feeling a bit uncomfortable since everyone around them seemed to have something to do. He wasn't happy just standing around and being waited on.

"Well, they're not from Earth obviously," Jackson began.

"No, really?"

Jackson ignored him. "But based on what the probe told us, their body chemistry is probably a lot like ours. Their houses are fascinating."

"Observe the children," Teal'C remarked in

the middle of the archaeologist's dissertation, studying the ebb and flow of the aliens gathering, talking, splitting into smaller groups, and then regathering as if they needed to touch each other constantly. "Or at least the smaller individuals. If they are indeed allowing children to participate in this event, it is unlikely they intend to harm us."

The little village swarmed with smaller versions of their three guides. The little ones behaved as apparently children did everywhere in the universe, with shy ones hanging back and braver ones running up to peer into the faces of the strange tall folk who had invaded their world. There was much giggling and teasing when the bravery ran out and the venturesome ones scurried away.

Carter got down on one knee, the better to deal with them on their own level, and laid her rifle on the ground beside her. O'Neill bit his tongue to keep from snapping at her for forgetting basic safety precautions, but the little one ignored the weapon and touched Carter's face with a featherlight, wondering caress, seeking the missing patterns of hair, touching her eyebrows as if relieved that there was something there after all.

Okay, he'd mention it to the major later. But she'd better not pull that stunt twice. The little guys were cute and all, but so were baby black widow spiders. Carter knew better than to let appearances deceive her.

"Children? Oh, yeah, but . . . that's not— Look at their clothing!" Jackson said. Fascinated, the team watched as some of the aliens' coverings changed shape into an approximation of fatigues, while on others, the material, whatever it was, remained static. The uninfluenced version of the clothing appeared to be layers of fabric in panels perhaps a foot wide, hanging from shoulders and hips, fluttering as the aliens moved. The little one communing with Carter touched her sleeve, and the gossamer tunic turned a dark, mottled green. The major took the newly colored material between her fingers and rubbed it lightly, awed. Both she and the child giggled at her reaction. Jackson, who was running the camcorder in wide sweeps to cover as much as possible, got the reaction shot and focused on the fabric in Carter's fingers.

It was obvious that the team was too tall to fit comfortably in any of the huts. As they watched, Silver and Red organized a clearing in the middle of the village, setting up tall poles to support a gauzelike shade that ran the length of the village square. They swept away most of the more noxious detritus of village life—they hadn't developed trash pickup yet on this world—and soon had wide reed mats spread out. Flat, meter-wide woven baskets heaped with various kinds of grain, fruit, vegetables—at least they looked like the familiar Earth foods—were placed at irregular intervals. Silver and Red walked around the perimeter of the shaded area, setting out shallow bowls full of incense that smouldered with a pleasant aroma, and the villagers began to settle along the edges of the mats. Rather than beginning to eat, however, they all looked at SG-1 expectantly.

Finally Brown rejoined the Earth team. "Come and eat," he invited them yet again. "Share our food."

"Hospitality always seems to involve sharing food, no matter where you are. Uh, it looks like they're not going to start until we join them," Jackson noted. Carter got back to her feet, picking up her rifle with a guilty start, and brushed herself off. The child, responding to a call from an older, or at least larger, individual, ran off.

"You guys go ahead," O'Neill said, letting go a deep breath. The aliens really did look benign. On the other hand, he'd heard *that* song before. "I'll stand watch."

"You're sure?" Jackson asked.

"Oh, yeah, I'm sure." Jack O'Neill had been caught once too often by seemingly innocuous food offered by aliens. He wasn't about to go through an experience like that one anytime soon—never, if he could avoid it.

Jackson, remembering the incident, nodded in understanding, but he was perfectly willing to take the risk himself. He sat down in the middle of the aliens and asked rapid-fire questions about everything, like a good anthropologist doing field research. He specialized in the "making peaceful contact" part of their mission, gathering data about new worlds and, while he was at it, finding out just how much contact such a world had with the Goa'uld.

So Teal'C and Carter settled down on the ground along the edge of the yellow reed mats with him, and O'Neill stood aside, watching, as the aliens offered them food that looked remarkably like apples and fist-size loaves of bread. No pomegranates, he noted, then wondered why he was obsessing on the subject. Brown looked at him, disappointed, and then sat down with the rest, apparently resigned to the idea that one of their visitors wasn't going to join the party.

Daniel accepted a jug of something liquid from one of the aliens and sipped. "Water," he said with some surprise and passed it along to Sam. The alien nodded.

"Tell us about your world," Daniel said between bites of apple. "We saw strange things and don't understand them."

The alien made a face that might have been a scowl or a smile—either way those teeth were awfully sharp—and passed along an extra apple to one of the kids (or smaller aliens) who was hanging around, wide-eyed and curious. O'Neill smiled at him, and the child offered him the apple, with one bite already taken out and disappearing between busy fangs. Those teeth didn't look vegetarian, but he couldn't see anything that looked like meat anywhere on the mats. In fact, the only cooked food seemed to be the bread. He wondered if they baked it inside their houses. He couldn't spot any exterior ovens.

The food looked good, and its odor was enhanced by the incense. O'Neill had grown out of his incense phase about thirty years previous, but this stuff actually did smell good, not overpowering at all. He could practically taste the flavor of the clear juices running from the fruit being held up to him. His stomach rumbled, and the child started, as if O'Neill had growled at him.

O'Neill glanced at Daniel, who usually was the arbiter of alien etiquette, but the blond scientist was deep in conversation with Brown. The kid nudged him again, persistently offering.

Well, if a child had already eaten from the fruit, it should—probably—be okay. He hoped. And he didn't want the kid to think he was mad at him. He took one small bite of the apple and returned it to the child, nodding.

He wasn't going to be allowed to discreetly spit it out. The kid was watching him eagerly, one three-fingered hand resting lightly on his belt. Wondering if he'd lost his mind O'Neill smiled again and chewed. Under the intent stare of the young one, he swallowed.

What he ate tasted exactly like an apple. A Granny Smith, to be exact. Tart and crisp and juicy. It was really good, in fact.

The kid bared its teeth in what O'Neill hoped was a smile and then scampered away, devouring the rest of the fruit as it went.

The meal went on, with O'Neill feeling more and more left out as his teammates engaged in animated conversations with the aliens around them. He kept a steady monitor on his own reactions as well as those of his team. If anyone started acting off, including himself, they were leaving instantly.

But nothing untoward occurred. He remained standing, feeling a bit bored, if anything. The only good thing about his self-appointed guardianship was that it allowed him to eavesdrop on everybody at once.

In response to Jackson's incessant questions, posed between mouthfuls, Silver said, "No, we are not the only ones here. There are others, but we, the Kayeechi, do not feast with them." He looked uncomfortable, and the nearest aliens shivered and fell silent for a moment.

"Are you at war?" Jackson asked, pushing the subject. "Do you fight with them?"

Silver, who had introduced himself as Shasee, looked around at the others as if seeking guidance. The others went on talking to each other as if the question had never been asked, but there was an air of unease about the place, and O'Neill was sure that they were all listening for the response.

"Yes," he said finally. "But this is not a time to discuss that. This is a celebration of visitors. War is an unpleasant topic."

That, at least, was indisputable, though O'Neill would have liked to have heard more nonetheless. However, his team seemed more inclined to tact than he was.

"Are there more Kayeechi living in other places?" Carter finally got a question in edgewise. Jackson took the opportunity to wash down a mouthful of bread and waited for the response.

The aliens looked at each other as if such a thing had never occurred to them. "Why would anyone want to live some other place than this?" Red asked, clearly confused. "We live *here*."

"So the others you don't feast with—the ones you fight—aren't Kayeechi?"

This earned Carter a look that implied she had an astounding grasp of the obvious. "Of course not," Shasee snapped, then relented, softening his tone. "We are a peaceful people. We don't fight among ourselves. We only fight others to defend ourselves when we have to."

"What about others that come through the Gate?" Teal'C asked some of the other small aliens crowded around the food. "Have you seen persons shaped like us?" Teal'C had not missed the implication: SG-1 would fall firmly into the category of "others" for this culture.

"Oh, no," he was assured. "We have never seen those like you before. We have tales of people who have come through the Hole In Nothing, but no one in this place has actually seen someone walk through it. Is it a most amazing place, the other side of Nothing?"

Even though these people had never heard of the Goa'uld, they had stories about someone using the Gate. And on top of that, they were engaged in local conflicts of their own. Ouch, O'Neill thought. Not good. Earth wasn't interested in taking sides in somebody else's wars, but they needed more information.

He wished they could just go ahead and *interrogate* the little guys, instead of Daniel's approach of laughing and joking and comparing his solid mass of yellow hair to the patch patterns of the aliens. It would certainly get information faster than the more casual and offhand approach that Jackson was using to pry more information about "someone using the Gate."

It would also probably alienate the aliens though. O'Neill held his patience and his tongue and let Jackson work, drawing on his professional expertise to sop up as much information as possible in the shortest time.

At least the Kayeechi didn't seem inclined to shoot strangers first and ask questions later. They appeared genuinely glad to meet the team from Earth, eager to talk to them. Maybe they really were peaceful.

"It's much like this place," Jackson said. "We live in cities. We have feasts. Sometimes we argue with our neighbors too."

"It is good to know that we are not so different," Shasee responded with an expression that was probably a smile. The supply of food was considerably reduced by now, and a few of the Kayeechi had risen from the mat and were taking away the empty serving dishes and scraping together the spare fruit. "Look. The suns are going down, and we have the ceremonial incense set up already. Let us welcome you properly with music and dancing, and you shall tell us more of the stories of your world."

It didn't seem to be a particularly harmful idea, and O'Neill agreed, thinking that this world, at least, was turning out to be relatively low stress, all things considered. The biggest problem was the little ones looking over their packs and weapons. Teal'C gently shooed the little ones away.

"What are these?" Brown asked.

"They're for our protection," O'Neill said bluntly. "We don't want anyone getting hurt, so we don't want you to touch them."

Brown smiled and put his hands behind his back, though he cast a longing look at the rifles and Teal'C's energy staff. Thenceforward, O'Neill and Teal'C were careful to keep their weapons out of sight, and provided no more information about their capabilities.

"Sir," Carter said, "I'm pretty sure the Kay-eechi have already guessed that 'the other side of Nothing' is another world, or at least very, very far away. Our appearance is very different from theirs, but that doesn't surprise them. They're taking it for granted that our clothing and packs are nothing like anything they have. That says to me that they've met others from far away."

"Agreed," said Jackson. "They've got stories about seeing people come through the Gate before." The natives were building a good-size bonfire out of the remains of the woven food platters and other odds and ends. "Not recently, but not Goa'uld either. I think we should see if we can identify who else might be using the Gates. They could be allies."

"Or enemies." Teal'C took the words right out of O'Neill's mouth.

Daniel ran a hand through his blond hair, the sign of too familiar exasperation with the military mind. "Or enemies, yes. But they don't seem to have a problem with people who come through the Gate, only with their surrounding neighbors. The usual territorial disputes over farming lands, and something they call *mor-ee*."

"What? Something that didn't translate?" O'Neill asked snidely, then reconsidered. "I heard you talking to them about the Gate earlier, but I missed this part. You have any idea what this *mor-ee* stuff is?"

Daniel shook his head. "Not yet. It could be something with ritual significance. It almost looks like they think we can help them with it."

"Absolutely not. Make that clear to them, Daniel. We're not getting into it. We're here to look for help for Earth. That's the primary mission, as you so kindly reminded me."

"I know. I've already said we aren't interested

in taking sides with anyone, but I'm not sure they accept it yet."

"Look, they're getting ready to light the—" Carter interrupted. "Whoa! Look at the colors!"

"Look at the damn smoke!" O'Neill snapped.

He was feeling unduly impatient, maybe because he was hungry while everybody else had gotten to eat already, and the smell of smoke made him even hungrier. Still, he had to admit that the smoke billowing from the bonfire was very pretty, in its own way—multiple colors, as if the fuel had been dampened with chemicals. He hadn't seen anyone adding anything suspect to the pile, but there was enough leftover food to account for it, and then of course the nature of the woven platters themselves. He blinked as a vagrant breeze blew the fragrant air into his eyes, and he tried to remember what he'd been talking about earlier. A dull throb of alarm went through him, then died away as he caught another lungful.

The scent of burning vegetable matter hung heavy on the air while the Kayeechi yelped and spun and sang and rattled metal together to make a tinny orchestral sound. The smoke made their eyes water, and Daniel sneezed, but no one remarked on any other effects. The dancers spun and hopped and followed an intricate invisible pattern around their visitors, and as each alien passed, it would hold out a clawed hand to one of the humans and beseech him or her to join in the dance. Teal'C, of course, had no problem refusing; the Jaffa was far too dignified to participate in such things, and besides, he was sniffing at the air as if seeking something that he couldn't quite remember.

Jackson and Carter each glanced at O'Neill before shaking their heads regretfully. After all, the dancing looked like fun; the dancers and the audience changed places at random or as the dancers tired and dropped out, laughing with their neighbors as they collapsed to the ground. Then one of the neighbors would jump up and join the line of gyrating, singing Kayeechians.

The humans watched, occasionally trying to pick up the rhythm of the song, bobbing along unconsciously when it approximated something they knew. The pleasure of their hosts was infectious. It was very hard to believe that they could possibly constitute anything like a threat.

However, SG-1 had long ago learned to believe six impossible things before breakfast, so they kept their eyes open as they kept time, and when Shasee made his way through the finally thinning crowd they were prepared for business.

"Tomorrow, we can bring you pictures of our other visitors," Shasee said as a few more diehards spun by. "Would you like to see them?

We have had many, many visitors here. Perhaps they are your friends."

"Pictures? We'd love to see them right now," Carter said instantly. "If you have pictures—"

"No, no. The pictures are not here. We have sent for them. You are our guests. Let us show you more of our land."

"Actually, it's getting kind of late," O'Neill started to decline. It was, in fact, getting very dark; there didn't seem to be any moons out to relieve the blackness of the sky. The idea of sleeping was wonderfully attractive somehow.

"Forgive us! Of course, you must rest. Come, let us take you to our guest camp, where you can be comfortable. Tomorrow we will talk more, and you will tell us all about your world and all the others who use the hole in the sky."

Jack closed his eyes and sighed. It would be better, he thought vaguely, for the team to set up its own camp away from the aliens, but they seemed so . . . friendly. And it would require so much effort, and he was so tired.

His brow furrowed a little as he struggled to grasp an odd feeling that there was something wrong about all this, but Shasee took him by the hand and tugged gently, and it was easier just to follow.

CHAPTER THREE

Shasee led the team to a quiet glen, close enough to still be able to hear the music from the party, but far enough away that it wasn't particularly disturbing. The clearing was bounded by a perimeter of small bronze dishes set in a loose circle perhaps fifty feet in diameter and a dozen feet apart; the air was permeated with the scent, not unlike cloves and cinnamon.

"What's this stuff?" O'Neill asked, indicating the smouldering dishes. Away from the bonfire, he was feeling not more alert, perhaps, but not quite as fuzzy. Or perhaps fuzzy in a different way. He felt for his sidearm just to make sure it was still there.

"It is to protect from insects," Shasee said blithely. "We have many night insects that bite. This keeps them away."

"Oh," the team chorused.

"In that case, thanks," Daniel added. The precaution made so much sense.

With that, Shasee skipped away, whistling cheerfully.

Daniel sneezed.

"Is this stuff going to give you trouble, buddy?" O'Neill asked him.

The archaeologist shook his head, then carefully drew a deep lungful of scented air and let it go. The breeze freshened and lifted the threads of smoke around them.

"No," he said at last. "I can see getting sick of the smell after a while, but I think I'm okay. It really isn't too bad. And we could always put a couple of these out, I guess, if it gets too bad."

"It reminds me of Christmas sugar cookies," Carter remarked. "Makes me hungry."

"Yeah, it does at that." At Teal'C's inquiring look, O'Neill shrugged. "A religious holiday. Lots of great food." O'Neill broke out a couple of Power Bars in lieu of an actual meal and settled down to chew, remembering the flavor of apple in his mouth. "Pies. Sweet potatoes. Roast beast. The good china."

Teal'C nodded, understanding. "The Jaffa celebrate such feasts, but they do not smell like this."

"You know," Carter said, staring into the small campfire, "we ought to have a Christmas party this year. We could hold it in the Officers' Club. Invite the general. Maybe some of his staff. Put up a tree." She glanced at Teal'C. "It's part of the celebration, decorating a tree with candy canes and popcorn and—"

"Will you please stop talking about food?" O'Neill groused. He was folding the wrappers into careful, precise little squares and tucking them back into his pack.

Carter grinned. "Yes, sir."

Having exhausted the subject of Christmas, they laid out a security perimeter and then set out bedrolls, with O'Neill claiming the first watch. The other three team members yawned and stretched out.

"Amazing place, isn't it?" Daniel said thoughtfully, staring into the new constellations that powdered the night sky. "Who could have imagined this kind of architecture? It's like those old comics of Space City I used to read about when I was a kid."

He didn't appear to notice his teammates staring at him as if he'd grown a third head.

"Did you get a load of that tower?" he went on. "It must be thirty stories— What? What's wrong?"

"Daniel," O'Neill said slowly, "what are you talking about?"

"The city. Where we just were. Where the Kayeechi live."

"There is no crystal tower," Teal'C stated definitively. "The dwellings in this village are built of thatch and hides. They represent a very limited use of tools."

"Are you nuts?" Now it was Carter's turn. "Granted, it's not the Jetsons, but it isn't Mud Holler either."

"Mud Holler?" O'Neill repeated, thoroughly confused.

What have you used in the pots?

What we always use, Most Thoughtful One. The mor'ee-rai.

They are not responding properly. They should have seen one shape. I called one single shape for them. How is it that these are different?

They came from Nothing.

They bring with them great powers. We need them. The Narrai are gathering, and there are too many of them this time.

The strangers will not go to sleep! They spend all their time talking to one another. In the council of the Kayeechi, the thoughts were wild with frustration. *They must sleep! How can I seek if they will not open their minds to me?*

What shall we do? The response was respectful, not cringing, not obsequious.

Take them to the Place of Dreams. They must *sleep tonight.*

Carter waved an impatient hand at her superior officer and sat up, looking at Teal'C and Jackson, who were staring back at her and at each other with nearly identical expressions of total confusion. "It looks a lot like a modern U.S. city," she said. "Okay, so there aren't any cars, but those houses were frame and stucco, and I saw a couple of brick facades." She turned to O'Neill in appeal. "Sir, what are they talking about?"

"Damned if I know," O'Neill said slowly. "On the other hand, I'm not sure that I know what you're talking about either. I didn't see any of that stuff. I saw tipis. And if we're really in some futuristic city, how come we're camping out under the trees?"

Jackson opened his mouth to reply and then shut it again, thoughtfully, staring at the team commander.

"We *do* all see trees around here, right?" he demanded.

"What trees?" Carter interrupted, clearly startled. "There aren't any trees around here. This is the middle of a city."

The three men stared at her.

"There aren't?" Daniel sputtered. "It is?"

"Oooooh-kay," O'Neill said quietly. "Carter, if there's a city around here, you're the only one who sees it. Or at least I think you are. Daniel, what do *you* see?"

"Gardens," the archaeologist responded promptly. "Formal gardens. Reminds me of Versailles. There's a building in the distance, but only one. It's white stone, about three stories tall. The crystal tower is somewhere behind it."

O'Neill blinked. "Teal'C?"

"Farmland," the Jaffa said. "I agree, there are no trees, but this is not a city. There are many small plots of land under cultivation, separated by wide dirt roads. We are standing on such a road as I speak."

All four looked down at their feet.

"That's not a dirt road, Teal'C," Carter said earnestly. "It's some kind of artificial surface. We're standing in the middle of a street. There's a big building with glass windows right over there." She lifted one hand to indicate what appeared to O'Neill to be a particularly large and spiky tree.

"That's topiary," Daniel said, bewildered.

"That is a farm cart," Teal'C contradicted.

"This is confusing," O'Neill summarized.

The four members of SG-1 stared at each other.

"Well, Colonel?" Carter said, with a clear this-is-why-you-earn-the-big-bucks air.

O'Neill closed his eyes and took a long breath. "I'm going to count to ten," he said quietly. "And when I reach ten, I'm going to open my eyes, and I'm going to be back home in bed. Right? One. Two. Three. Four—" His eyes snapped open.

He wasn't home in bed, but Shasee stood before him, grinning up apologetically. His teammates were still there too, all of them looking around, comparing all too contradictory notes.

"So very sorry," Shasee repeated for the third or fourth time. "This is not where you are supposed to be after all, after all. Let me take you, honored visitors, to a safe sleeping place."

"Unless I get some answers right now, the only place we're going is back to the Gate and home." O'Neill detached a silver-furred, three-digit hand from his arm and glared down at the little alien. "Shasee, why do we all see different things here?"

"Mistake, mistake. Confusion, oh, terrible confusion." Red, who was named Vair, joined his fellow. "This is not the place to sleep. This is the wrong place. Come with us to the right place."

"Uh, you brought us here to begin with," Daniel pointed out to Shasee. "Why is it the wrong place all of a sudden?"

"We did not know you could see the shapes,"

Vair answered. "All see different shapes. Yes, you do—not good. We need to fix the shapes. Much less confusing."

"Are you projecting images into our minds?" Daniel asked.

The two aliens looked at each other as if the question were as confusing as the circumstances the team found itself in.

O'Neill watched the two natives struggle with the question and its answer and relaxed infinitesimally. He still got no sense that the Kayeechi were a threat to himself or his people, even if the differing realities each of them perceived could be deadly dangerous if they needed to defend themselves.

He was of two minds about the situation. One part of him had definitely decided to haul ass back home, out of this place where no two of them could agree on what they were looking at. The other was wildly curious about it all and insisted that nothing they'd seen looked like it would hurt them.

Well, that roc maybe.

But they'd *all* seen the roc. Maybe they should have asked some questions about that at the party.

"Confusion," Vair responded finally. "All is confusing. We are so sorry. Please come to a place not confusing."

"I'm all for that." O'Neill was glad to gather up his little band and follow the Kayeechai to a new location, temporarily postponing the whole issue. They left the glen and followed a path—everyone agreed on that much. Up a little hill—yes, they had concensus there too—to their new location.

"Okay, Vair, Shasee. What is this place we're in now? How is it different from where we were before?"

Vair lit torches set in walls, providing a pleasant, if not overbright, level of illumination.

"This is a safe place," Shasee said earnestly. "This is the Place of Dreams, where you can rest safely. Please. Rest. Sleep. Accept our apologies."

O'Neill hiked a skeptical eyebrow.

Vair and Shasee withdrew, still assuring them that this new location was, "A good place, a safe place."

Once the aliens were gone, the four team members looked around cautiously.

"Cave?" asked O'Neill.

"Cave," confirmed Teal'C.

Carter and Jackson were also convinced that their new camp was in a cave, or at least a shallow depression in the side of the little hill. The place was deep enough that the far end would have been in permanent darkness if it hadn't been for the aromatic torches that flared from the wall sconces. The floor had been swept clean of rocks and debris and there were no signs of previous residents likely to take exception to the newcomers.

O'Neill wasn't satisfied. "I'm not happy about this," he said, "but I'm not unhappy enough yet to turn tail and run. Tomorrow morning, we're heading back to the Gate."

"Why not just review the field tapes and find out which one of us was right?" Carter asked.

"Brilliant," Jackson said, and without waiting for orders, he pulled out the camcorder and hit the PLAYBACK button.

The tape was blank.

"Oh, now that's just not fair!"

"It looks like the tape got exposed—"

"It puts us exactly where we were five minutes ago," O'Neill said. "And we've been in lots worse places—I think. Get some sleep. I've still got first watch."

Daniel sneezed again. O'Neill glanced at him and then at the torches set a meter or so apart in the walls of the cave.

"Those torches aren't going to do much for my night sight. I'm going to put most of them out. Any objections?"

The others shook their heads and once again set out bedrolls while O'Neill tamped down one torch after the next. Short of total immersion in their water supply, which was not an option, he couldn't stop them from smoking, but at least they weren't burning with an open flame anymore and the glare was considerably lessened. His night sight gradually improved as the flames went out. He left one torch lit at the very back of the cave just for reassurance.

Somewhat reassured, the three subordinate members of the team stretched out to sleep while a still confused O'Neill sat a few yards in from the mouth of the little cave and looked out into the darkness. The light of the single torch was so dim that he couldn't even distinguish his own shadow.

If mere confusion were a good reason to abort a mission, he thought, then this one would have been toast the moment the trees started walking. But the thing about alien worlds was that they were, well, *alien*. So far, nothing sentient had tried to hurt them.

Or had it and the Earth team simply didn't see it?

Probably not, he decided. They'd all seen the same things, only different versions of buildings and landscape and whatnot. His gut said they were all right here. Whatever threat there was didn't seem to be directed at them personally.

He got up, stepping softly over a snoring Jackson, and walked noiselessly to the mouth of the cave and a couple of steps outside. They'd all agreed it was a cave, but who knew what kind of cave each of them saw? He was going to double-check the camcorder in the morning to make sure it was running properly. He hadn't met the alien yet that could make a machine hallucinate.

Behind him, Carter stretched and muttered in her sleep, and O'Neill allowed himself a smile. Whatever the major was dreaming about, it sounded like fun. The torches were smoking even more now, giving off a not unpleasant scent. He could smell it clearly, even standing outside the cave entrance and looking upward.

The moonless night sky was velvety, spangled and powdered with stars in unfamiliar constellations. Wondering which ones he ought to know, he shook his head. One dot of light was much like another, and lacking a spectral analysis, he could only identify them by their relationship with each other, and then only from Earth as a reference point. It was a big universe out there.

And *he* got to walk in it.

"Cool," he murmured, and suddenly one of the constellations stepped closer.

He blinked. He hadn't seen anything like that since the Seventies. Or maybe since Apophis had made him the Blood of Sokar—except that this time, he wasn't seeing Charlie, and oh, yes, his leg wasn't killing him.

Apophis was *dead*. Whatever was going on here was something else.

A line of treetops, blacker against the black of the night, began to sway seductively in a hula rhythm. Above them, the stars danced.

He took one step back, deeper into the cave, and the trees stilled.

One step forward. The trees were just trees.

"This is crazy," he told himself. If the cave was protected by some kind of antihallucination force field, how come he wasn't hallucinating now?

On the horizon, light blossomed, not like an explosion but like the glow of a city that moments before hadn't been there. As he studied it, the light changed colors, and tiny specks zipped through it in orderly lines, as if under the benign dictatorship of an air-traffic controller.

A meteorite shower maybe?

He stepped back again, and the light faded.

"Shoulda had something more to eat," he said and began searching through his pack for a candy bar. He'd have Janet check his blood-sugar levels when they got back. He was starving, suddenly.

"Hungry?" It was Shasee. He hadn't heard the little silver-furred alien approach, and for a moment, that was cause enough for alarm. But Shasee was holding out an armful of fruit, much like the apple he had sampled earlier, and some-how it was only logical that he should have some more. Shasee nodded and made smiling faces as O'Neill devoured the food. As if the taste itself created more hunger, he couldn't get enough of it.

Behind him, his team slept on peacefully.

Eventually sated, he joined them.

In the Kayeechi village, several small anxious aliens gathered under the shelter, casting wary eyes as they came. They crowded around the four in the center of their circle and waited in breathless silence.

Finally, the thoughts said desperately, and the observers stirred in agreement. *Now let us see what our visitors shape for us.*

But it was too late for shaping.

Etra'ain! came a panicked mental cry. *Etra'ain! The Narrai are moving closer!*

Go and meet them, the response came. *Drive them away with lesser shapes. We must take the op-portunity offered now. It may not come again.*

There were moans of terror, but the observers obediently scattered, leaving the four sur-rounded by smudge pots, staring into each other's eyes and each other's thoughts, reaching for other realities. Shaping.

CHAPTER FOUR

With a jolt, Jack O'Neill found himself in Iraq, under a blazing sun, bellied up to a sand dune and looking down at a small green spot in the desert that meant "water here." In this case it also meant one of Saddam's underground germ factories. His assignment was to take it out.

He had been here before.

That spot of green—and it shouldn't be that vivid: Iraq wasn't all sand dunes and rocks after all—was close up, much closer than it had been a moment before. He was within scaling distance of the wall.

He looked around for his team.

Teal'C.

Teal'C, wearing desert cammies, with a military-issue rifle and sidearm and a belt full of grenades, the mark on his forehead— No, wait. It had only seemed to catch the sun, but it was gone now. Teal'C was watching him, waiting for the signal.

As soon as he gave the signal, the two of them would swarm past the hidden checkpoint through the little village, force their way into the dilapidated mud building, and find themselves in a modern laboratory filled with purification vats and filters and all manner of stuff used to purify and replicate viruses: anthrax, HIV, things with the incubation period and infectiousness of the common cold and the deadliness of Ebola.

It made perfect sense for Teal'C to be here. Some part of O'Neill knew that there were supposed to be others—he wasn't supposed to do this alone—he had been hurt . . .

No, the thought said with agitation. *Not this time. I need something else.*

Outside the disguised lab building, he could see a heavy stake driven into the ground. Tied to it was the body of a young chimpanzee, lying in a puddle of fluids and covered with a mantle of flies—a test subject.

It seemed logical to test a virulent biological weapon in the middle of the town used to disguise the presence of the laboratory, right in front of the target building.

Not far away, three women in black gowns sat, their faces uncovered since only women were present, gabbing away as they threaded something on strings.

A little boy raced past, screaming, chasing a young brown goat.

Teal'C was waiting.

O'Neill waved him in and took off himself at a low, ground-eating run, his rifle heavy in his hands. He could feel the metal against the palms of his hands, a sensual chill and weight that nearly distracted him from his target.

The women, surprised, turned to look at him. They exclaimed to each other as they hastily covered their faces, but made no move to escape or avoid him.

He could hear Teal'C beside him, behind him, his footsteps thudding heavily against the hard ground as they gave the dead chimpanzee a wide berth by common consent. The two of them headed for the door and planted themselves on either side.

There was no sound from the inside. The women were still whispering and giggling to each other, making the little head movements that meant they were pointing with their chins to indicate the two invaders. O'Neill was puffing hard—out of shape, bad news on a mission. His glance fell on the body of the chimp, with smears of blood at every orifice and lips skinned back from long, businesslike teeth. It hadn't been an easy death. It wasn't one that O'Neill would wish on anybody, even Saddam.

Well, maybe Saddam.

He and Teal'C communicated with quick glances that gave directions about who was high, who was low, which direction to sweep fire. He took a deep breath and looked up to see that an audience had gathered before the building: women and children. Mostly children.

He shook his head and waved the rifle at them, trying to warn them to get out of the way. But they laughed and applauded.

If they weren't careful, they were going to get those kids killed. Like Charlie. No, there he was standing in the front row with the rest of them, his blond head making him stand out from the others but part of them nonetheless. O'Neill waved at his son—his dead son—to stay back because he could get hurt. He couldn't stand it if Charlie got hurt again.

He had come home early and was nuzzling Sara in the garden when he heard the report of the gun. He knew the sound of that gun as well as he knew the sound of his son's voice. He knew what had happened. He could still feel the stab of the icicle in his heart as if it were happening all over again: the glimpse of movement in the corner of his eye that was his son ducking out of the way the day he'd put the gun away. Charlie loved to watch his daddy cleaning it, loved to play with the gun oil and cotton patches and make a mess, but Daddy never showed him where the gun was kept, up on the very top shelf out of the reach of inquisitive fingers, but there had been that movement. He was a smart kid. He'd figured it out. All the warnings, all the patient explaining counted for nothing—and here they were, a crowd of kids watching the grown-ups play with guns, and now they descended on the two men like a pack of ferrets, reaching for the deadly toys.

No. Wait. Something was wrong.

"Teal'C? What the hell are *you* doing here?"

Abruptly, Teal'C was gone, and he was lying still—so very still, trying not to breathe, trying to play dead, to *be* dead. Frank had to come back for him and get him out. The Iraqis were all around him, standing over him, watching for any signs of life, and suddenly he couldn't stand it anymore. He reached for his boot knife and felt the metal hilt against his hand as he had felt the weight of the rifle.

No, the thoughts said. *Useless against so many. Try something else.*

And now he was in a cage, and the Iraqis stood around and poked at him through the bars.

And the one in particular who always smiled at him, the teeth white against the black beard.

"Confess, American dog."

"That is *so* old-fashioned—"

So was a cattle prod, but it worked nonetheless. He screamed and his back arched high. They gathered around him and laughed, kicking him.

What do you use? You are alone, one against many. What can you use?

Submachine gun.

It appeared in his suddenly unbound hands, and he pulled the trigger in one long burst, spraying upward at the grinning faces. Firing straight up.

What goes up must come down with equal velocity.

His own bullets killed him.

No. Something else.

It is a powerful weapon.

It strikes back at itself. There must be something else.

Back in the desert. It was the seventh day of hell, but he was still moving. He could feel ribs grinding together; he took short, shallow breaths, panting to keep from expanding his fractured rib cage. He didn't want to look behind himself, because he was pretty sure he would see an O'Neill-wide path of blood across the sharp rocks of the wadi.

At the moment, he was nose to nose with a small grayish-brown snake. It hissed, and he could see venom running from the fangs, dripping to the sand.

"If you bite me, son, you're gonna be the sorriest snake in the Middle East," he breathed, and held very, very still.

The snake hesitated, holding at least a third of its body in the air, and jabbed. He could feel the push of displaced air against his face.

He held still.

He could feel the sharp point of a rib trying to probe its way through his skin and out his side.

The snake tasted the air. It had to smell him. Hell, *he* could smell him after seven days of crawling across the Iraqi desert. His parachute had provided silk to splint his leg together, but the blood had soaked through. Sweat was running into his eyes, and through the stubble of his beard. He had an almost irresistible urge to sneeze from the dust caked around his nose and mouth. Air flowed softly, quietly past parched lips, down his throat, into his barely stirring lungs.

The snake decided O'Neill was too big to eat and slithered away.

His head dropped to the sand, and he groaned.

Not useful.

The snake was back suddenly, as if time had clicked backward several frames—only this time his side didn't hurt so much and he had an automatic in his hand. He managed somehow to pull back the slide and point it at the snake. The barrel wandered back and forth with the shaking of his hand, and the snake's head began to follow it.

He pulled the trigger, and missed.

Useless! Something else!

Perhaps a different place?

He fired a flare to signal the choppers to land. They were coming in low, having dumped a load of defoliant over Colombian poppy fields. The arch of light hissed through the sky, bringing them home.

They are coming in from the skies. Is there any way to stop them in the sky?

The thunder of the rotors came closer, blowing dust into his eyes, whipping at the hair on his head and the clothes on his body. He held up an arm to protect his sight, and the Huey settled to the earth right next to him.

That could be—

Look closer. It isn't a weapon.

Does it matter if we can use it?

Can we use it?

They're coming! They're coming—many of them! Etra'ain, help us!

The circle of Shapers broke as the Narrai swept through the homes of the Kayeechi. The first of them landed on the roof beam of the tallest building and spread his wings to their full span, balancing, as the rest of them tore through the place. The Kayeechi poured out of their homes, some trying to strike back and some seeking shelter under trees. The wings of the Narrai were so large they had difficulty negotiating through the boughs. Their wings were their deadliest weapons, smashing roofs and walls like tinder, while the Kayeechi used bows and staffs in a largely futile effort to beat them off.

The Narrai sent their long necks twisting and turning through the wreckage of the buildings, seeking the little ones of the Kayeechi, snapping them up. Some they swallowed immediately; others they chopped in half with the great beaks; a few they transferred from beak to clawed foot to carrying pouch. One or two managed to scramble free of the pouches, only to fall to the ground, dazed and wounded. The Kayeechi brought out fire arrows and torches to burn the houses, depriving the Narrai of their perches. Two of the gigantic birds twisted and screamed as the arrows penetrated flesh; one toppled to the ground, where the Kayeechi swarmed upon it with axes, chopping it to pieces while it thrashed. Several of the Kayeechi were flung through the air by the desperate flailing, but each time they were replaced, and finally one of the axes found a vulnerable spot in the throat and the bird screamed out a fountain of blood before shuddering into stillness. Another swooped down beside it, only to have another ax bury itself in the massive wing joint; it shrieked and collapsed. The others hovered over it, but the arrows came in black clouds now, and four Kayeechi managed to heave the weighted ends of a net over the crippled flier.

The Narrai finally fell back, hissing, before the fire arrows and long torches of the humanoids. The sounds of screaming echoed over the hills and trees.

The raid was as brief as it was sudden. Less than an hour after they had been first detected, the Narrai were rising in the air, beating their way back to their aeries, leaving the Kayeechi and their single fatality in a midnight shambles behind them.

Vair, Shasee, and Eleb, the leaders of the Council of Kayeechi, stood in the middle of the smoking ruins and looked around them. Nearby, a wounded mother dragged herself free of the debris of a wall. Her child lay just outside, its guts spilled from a gaping wound that had just missed killing it instantly. The canopy beneath which they had feasted with their alien visitors was reduced to three and a half wooden posts thrusting charred splinters into the sky. The three of them reeked of smoke and blood.

"May their eggs shatter," Eleb the brown muttered. "We should have destroyed their nests when we had the chance."

"Yes," Vair said through clenched fangs. "We can Shape and Shape, but until we destroy them it will do us no good. We have to carry the battle back to them and finish them before they finish us."

"What we have to do now," Shasee said firmly, "is Shape shelter for our people. We will let Etra'ain seek a way to win. Meanwhile, we have work of our own to do."

Eleb sighed in agreement.

The three of them stood shoulder to shoulder and stared at the crumbled wall. Mother and dead child had been moved out of the way as the others saw what their leaders were about.

As they stared at the wall and Remembered what it had been like, the fallen timbers and stones and cloth trembled.

And rose.

And reassembled themselves.

The three breathed shallowly, Remembering

the wall whole. Behind them the survivors gathered, watching, Remembering too.

The smell of burning vanished with the charring, the smoke, the signs of utter destruction. The little crowd of Kayeechi, united, remembered what it had been before, only hours ago, before the Narrai came.

Before them, the house stood whole again. Eleb stepped up to it and touched it lightly with his hand, then hit it as hard as he could. The wall stood firm. He rubbed at the sore spot on his hand.

The trio of leaders and the little crowd moved on to Remember the next house, and the next, removing the dead and injured each time before they began to Shape the houses exactly as they had been before, minus the dead inhabitants.

And elsewhere, Etra'ain and her circle gathered once again to stare into the minds of the visitors from Nothing.

Something else. We must find something else. We must.

Try another. Surely one of them has something we can use.

CHAPTER FIVE

Teal'C had been raised to believe the Goa'uld were gods: omnipotent, omniscient, immortal.

One was not supposed to hate one's gods.

After a while he had realized they were not gods—not really. They were parasites, and their stolen host bodies could bleed and die just as his own could if the damage was more than the parasite or a handy sarcophagus could heal.

But they were still more powerful than anything else he had seen. He served bitterly, hiding his resentment, his rage at the bondage of himself and his people, because the Goa'uld could not be defeated. He was good at hiding his feelings, so good that he had advanced steadily until he was Jaffa First, the most trusted servant of Apophis. Even in his hatred Teal'C felt pride in that achievement; he had never seen any world that had anything like a chance against the Goa'uld, his masters.

Never, that is, until the day that a man looked at him across a scene of carnage and yelled, "I can save these people!"

He had believed Jack O'Neill. He had turned his energy staff against his own troops and defected to the sworn enemies of Apophis.

So what was he doing here, surrounded by Jaffa in their serpent helmets and waiting for orders with the rest of them?

He could feel the infant Goa'uld within him curl around itself.

He looked around as he lifted his own helmet torc over his head. The place was familiar, the kind of familiarity that meant he belonged in this place. He'd been here so many times before he never noticed the detail.

He noticed them now—burnished metal walls the color of dark copper, twisted columns that were more embellishment than any real structural necessity. It was a Jaffa briefing room, and that low, soundless vibration he could feel through his feet and in his bones meant that he was on board a Goa'uld mothership.

The Jaffa moved past him, dozens of them, and assembled themselves in orderly ranks facing him, standing at attention. They were waiting upon his pleasure, waiting for his orders.

He was back with Apophis, and though he could remember everything about his time with

SG-1, he could not remember how he had ended up here. It didn't seem important, and yet it had to be, because if Apophis had him he should be dead, not preparing to brief his troops as he had done so many times before.

There were so *many* Jaffa standing before him.

Then, exactly as if he had indeed provided yet another detailed briefing on the objectives of Apophis's most current desire, the assembled Jaffa saluted him, fists hitting leather breastplates like dull, simultaneous heartbeats. They pivoted and filed out past him, their booted feet heavy against the deck plates, and as they did so, he could feel the ship poised to land, the slight shudder as it settled on its resting place. They carried their energy staffs proudly.

What is this?

Something. Useful?

The image changed, and he was leading a troop of Jaffa into a large auditorium. A crowd of frightened humans huddled in the center of the room, and Apophis walked behind him, arrogant and proud but not willing to stand in front of his warriors.

One of the humans stooped and picked up a rock—what was a rock doing indoors?—and threw it. It ricocheted off Teal'C's helmet and bounced off the arm of the Jaffa next to him.

"Kill them all," Apophis said.

"My lord," Teal'C began a protest, knowing even as he did so that it was not only futile but dangerous to oppose his Goa'uld lord.

"Kill them all." The Goa'uld's voice echoed in basso profundo, shaking the very floor they stood upon.

Resigned, Teal'C leveled his energy staff and began to fire long sweeping beams of energy that caught and flattened their human targets like wheat under a scythe.

This! This we can use!

Can we ask? This is the staff he carries now.

A snort of derision. To possess a weapon was one thing; to ask for one was . . . ridiculous. Strangers did not give away power. It was unheard of.

But in the Shaping, one could examine such power, study it. Move the witless dreamers to demonstrate it . . . and make it real.

Let us see more of this.

He found himself in the Jaffa armory, running a soft cloth the length of the energy staff, checking the slide of the triggering mechanism, examining the way the bulbous head of the staff separated to spit out death. It was power, the power of the Jaffa—power of the Goa'uld.

He marched at the head of his chosen troops into yet another city, another auditorium. He stood at attention while Goa'uld chose those who would receive the matured larvae, menaced the crowd, chased those who would flee, executed those who dared oppose. This was his life, and he lived through it helplessly, knowing how it would be even if he himself had never been there. It pulled him along to his final fear: There was nothing, anywhere, that could stand against the Goa'uld.

In some universes, it had actually happened that way.

He had killed himself—or at least another self—to prevent it.

He had claimed that this reality was the one that counted. But the symbiote within him fought back in its own mindless fashion, creating something else.

He entered the Gate room through the Stargate, the iris spinning back out of the way as if it had never been there, and the place was so familiar: the ramp, the guards standing by, the computers calculating the location of the next set of coordinates and how far they might have shifted in thousands of years. When he raised his head he could see the viewing window from the humans' briefing room, and staring down at him in turn was General Hammond, his face perfectly impassive as Teal'C led the Jaffa through the Gate and into the heart of the human command complex.

They screamed as they looked up from their tasks and saw the invading Jaffa, their helmets' eyes glowing red, and someone managed to hit an alarm before dying under the relentless fire of energy staffs. The main door to the room slid open and human soldiers poured through, scrambled to meet the threat, but they weren't ready. Some were in uniform, rifles at the ready, but some were half dressed and struggling into flak jackets that did them no good under the withering fire of the disciplined Jaffa.

Teal'C had known the humans would not be ready; after all, the iris had let him through. His Jaffa had fanned out from the Gate immediately, denying the defenders a tight target. The alarms screamed and lights flashed, but he led his squad through the humans like a spear, securing the door before they had a chance to lock it down, and then the Jaffa began hunting through the corridors of the Stargate complex.

Carter died first, her eyes wide and unbelieving even as she fired steadily at him from a prone position in the command corridor. Her bullets couldn't touch him, couldn't touch any of his men. They mowed down the opposition, and as he stepped over Carter's body, her eyes were still wide and unbelieving, but dead.

Hammond was next. He led his men unerringly to the command offices, even as the humans threw more and more men and firepower against them; he knew that more and more Jaffa were pouring through the Gate to meet them, the two waves crashing against each other in a fountain of human—never Jaffa—blood. Hammond stood beside his desk, unarmed, alone, waiting for his fate. Did he expect the courtesies which were the right of opposing commanders? Probably not, Teal'C thought, as one of his squad aimed and fired and then snapped the energy rod back up again in parade rest. Hammond staggered back, half turned, fell across his desk, then back behind it without making a single sound.

The sound of Jaffa boots echoed everywhere in the mountain as he led his men from one room to the next, methodically wiping out the opposition as if the humans had never had any weapons at all. He could hear explosions, flashes of energy, unending gunfire, but he kept on through all the noise and smoke as if it were nothing at all. He moved at a steady trot, from one precise target to the next: the infirmary, where Janet Frasier died defending her patients. Central research office, where he found Daniel Jackson and swept him aside like so much lint from a woolen tunic. He kept moving, his nostrils flaring as he hunted, killed, hunted again.

"I can save these people!"

No, Jack O'Neill, you cannot save them. They are the victims of the Goa'uld, and nothing is as powerful as the Goa'uld. Nothing.

What? What thought is that?
That is the mind of the dreamer, the voice of despair. This is an evil weapon.
Weapons are neither good nor evil. They are tools, and we need tools.
But we need to see him use it again.
Something is in the way. I do not understand. This is a mind and . . . something else.
Watch. Observe.
Shape.

The Jaffa swept through a monitoring station, and Teal'C paused long enough to scan the external views of the mountains—fighters massing against the Goa'uld ship like so many mosquitoes battering themselves against the stone of an ancient pyramid. As he watched, a jet crashed directly against the slanted side of the Goa'uld ship. The burning wreckage, black oily clouds and orange flames consuming it, slid down the side without so much as denting the alien ship, without marring its perfect surface.

He turned and led his squad out of the room without bothering to look at the monitors again. Targets. They were all targets: the command center, the research office, the infirmary, the barracks. They broke out of the Stargate Command complex and into the interior of the Cheyenne Mountain complex. It was a waste of good slaves, all this killing, but Earth was full of slaves waiting for their masters, and they made their way out of the mountain, and as he had expected, as he had always secretly feared, the humans really were unable to resist.

Around him, the Jaffa cascaded down the sides of the mountain from the Goa'uld ship, millions and millions of serpent-headed men, a murderous avalanche overwhelming the world.

"I can save these people!"

Perhaps. But soon there would be only the dead to save.

Is it enough?

It is never enough. Investigate further. Plumb each to their depths. Find every detail of their weapons. The Narrai keep coming, and we have no one else here to take dreams from.

CHAPTER SIX

A large archaeological excavation can resemble a small city of tents and workers gathered to recover the evidence of a more ancient city of clay. Daniel Jackson threaded his way through the tents and stepped over the first of the twine boundaries that defined the dig's grid system. Every three feet, a stake anchored the twine, creating carefully defined squares. Some of them had already been excavated down several layers, and sifting screens beside them gave evidence that every scrap of dirt had been examined for artifacts.

It was a familiar sight. He smiled. These were the signs of a well-organized dig. Without even looking, he knew that the site notes would be neat and precise and informative. He'd grown up with archaeology, lived and breathed it all his life. He knew without thinking about it how to step carefully along the paths defined as clear, how to recognize the subtle lift of the earth's surface that meant that centuries before, that earth had been disturbed by man. He didn't even notice the heat and glare of the sun, high in the sky.

No one seemed to be around, but the time of day might account for that; it was easier to work in the early hours, before the temperature rose into three digits, and in the early evening, while there was still light enough to see. In the middle of the day—well, the phrase "only mad dogs and Englishmen go out in the noonday sun" did have its applications.

Still, there were usually at least a couple of overenthusiastic graduate students hunched down by the remains of an ancient hearth, using soft camel-hair brushes to patiently coax dirt away from a potsherd. He couldn't see anyone around the ruins.

What ruins *were* these anyway? He paused to study them for a moment, trying to orient himself. He could see low, crumbled walls, the remains of mud-brick architecture. In his mind's eye he could see those walls whole again, containing tiny rooms where people once lived and laughed. They had walked along these paths, bargained for food and other necessities, danced and celebrated and loved life, mourned and buried their . . .

. . . dead.

What is this?

He thinks this is his life. But this is a place of death. I don't understand.

Perhaps there will be something here to help us bury our own dead. You are bitter, Vair.

!

Very well. Are the survivors gathered and counted? How are they shaped?

There are not many of us left. We cannot survive if we cannot destroy the Narrai at their nests. They will come again and again and again until we are all dead. Etra'ain, we must find a way!

I continue to seek.

Slowly he turned, and found that the city of tents had disappeared and had been replaced by a massive pyramid, larger than Kheops's, larger than any pyramid he had ever seen. The sides had been finished and were smooth and white, dazzling in the bright sunlight. Not far from where he stood awed, a ramp rose up along the side of the massive structure, a wooden path from the sullen earth to a large rectangular defect in the sloping side. It had to be an entrance— the original entrance, not one that a later scientist had created to gain access to the interior. He caught his breath in sheer wonder.

The next moment he was inside the main entry shaft of the pyramid, with no memory of climbing the ramp or moving from bright sunlight into darkness. And that was strange too, because even though it was dark, he could still see. He ran his fingertips over the outlines of the massive stones, feeling the ancient marks of chisel and human sweat.

The tunnel angled downward steeply, and he had to move slowly to keep his balance, stooping as he walked; the ancient Egyptians had been shorter, as a rule, than their descendants. More than once he had to edge around a pit that would have swallowed him up, but each time he managed to pass it safely.

The pictures on the wall described his journey, described the journey of the deceased: Beloved of Horus, Osiris, Great Lord of the Dead, He Who Holds Justice in Both Hands. The colors were fresh and clear as the day they were painted.

As he descended, the sides of the shaft grew wider, the ceiling higher, and the sourceless light intensified. Unlike the desert sunlight, however, this light brought no warmth with it, and he shivered in his light cotton shirt and shorts and murmured to himself as he straightened. But he could no more abandon the exploration than he could stop breathing. He could feel a faint urge to stop, to do something else, but this was what he was born for, and no trivial tugging at his mind and memory was going to distract him.

He knows this place. He seeks truth here.

Truth is not a weapon to kill Narrai!

You are afraid, and we understand, Vair. But this path may give us information of value as well. Let us see where it takes us.

Despite the open entrance, it seemed that no one had ever entered this tomb since the days that its occupant had been laid to rest by singing priests. As the tunnel finally leveled out, the dust on the floor rose up in pale puffs with each footstep. He should have needed some kind of breathing filter, something to keep the ancient talc out of his lungs, but somehow it didn't bother him. His right foot kicked something more solid than dust, and he looked down to see a model ship, complete with papyrus sail and tiny oars. It looked new, or it would have if the hull hadn't collapsed under the blow. The rim of the boat was trimmed in gold foil.

The room was full of furniture, in fact: chairs with arms carved to represent wings; headrests for sleeping (and how did they manage to sleep that way? It looked awfully uncomfortable, and the one time he'd tried it himself, with a modern reproduction, he'd gotten a crick in his neck that took weeks to work out—so much for devotion to science); stands to support the great ostrich fans that kept desert air circulating; beds; a full-size chariot needing only a pair of horses and a driver to take off across the desert in pursuit of antelope or Hittites. Everything the well-to-do corpse would need in the afterlife.

He kept going. According to all the old pyramid plans, the shaft ought to angle upward, and there should be a plug blocking the entrance to the main burial chamber, but he found no obstructions. He wondered why all the scientists and students laboring outside had never bothered to venture up the ramp and inside. It was dangerous, entering a tomb, but surely someone would have tried? Surely he wasn't the only one curious enough to venture deep into the unknown?

So much the better if he was; that meant this was all his own discovery, his alone.

Of what possible use is this? Old bones and trash!

Wait. It is more than that. This is something old of his world, and there may be things of use—

Besides, there was something—someone—waiting for him at the end of this tunnel. Someone he wanted very much to see. He moved forward even more eagerly than before, knowing that the lack of barriers was a message to him, telling him that someone was waiting just for him.

The passage turned abruptly, and he found

himself in a chamber filled with weapons of ancient Egypt: bows, spears, bronze knives, slingshots lining the walls as they might in an armory.

This wasn't right. Pharoahs never filled their tombs with weapons of war. He looked around in disgust, then turned back, and the passage reopened before him.

It turned a corner, and he found himself in the armory again.

"This is *not* where I want to be," he said to himself and pushed through the limestone wall, looking for the stone tunnel again.

His path was littered with Hyksos war clubs. He kicked them aside impatiently and picked up his pace, almost running now.

Where is he going? Bring him back!

I cannot. I have not created this dream, and I cannot keep him under tight control in it—

Then the passage opened out into a room, a cavern almost, and the light from nowhere brightened until he could see the paintings on the walls, fresh and vibrant: images from the Book of the Dead in which the occupant of this tomb met the gods, had his heart weighed against the white feather of truth, answered questions about how he had lived his life while the gods looked on, Thoth recording, Osiris presiding, Anubis the black jackal standing by. The images on the walls were represented by statues lining the sides of the room, along with representations of the Pharoah buried here, wearing the double crown of Egypt and the false beard of authority, carrying the scepter and flail crossed over his chest. Daniel looked for the hieroglyphs that would tell him the name of the dead king, but he couldn't find them. Unusual. Unthinkable, in fact. Recording the name of the deceased was one of the ways to ensure its immortality. The name and titles should be everywhere.

The silence was more stifling than the millennia-old atmosphere. He scraped his feet along the floor for the sake of the noise. It echoed in the large room, and he stopped doing it, self-conscious about the effort.

The large room was only the anteroom, of course. The actual burial chamber—which should have been blocked and was not—was much smaller. Here too the walls were painted, but the images were hard to see, obscured behind even more neatly stacked paraphernalia of the afterlife that a royal personage would require: tables, figures of servants, horses, vases, food—it was still fresh! The millet still smelled of the field; the olives were still damp. He picked up a lamp and heard the slosh of oil, set it down again on a table carved ready for a game. It was amazing. He might have stepped back into the days when the tomb was first opened for its occupant.

Still, no matter how rich or fresh the furnishings, only one thing mattered here.

And there it was, overwhelming, in the center of the room: the sarcophagus, easily four feet high, solid gold, inlaid with enamels and precious stones, shaped and painted in the image of the dead, kohl-lined eyes staring serenely at the clouds painted on the ceiling. A line encircling the stone showed where the lid fitted tightly to the base.

He set his hands on the edge of the sarcophagus and hesitated. The thing must weigh more than a ton, but who knew what might be inside?

Was this the one he had hastened to meet?

The massive lid moved easily, if loudly, under his hands, scraping and shifting and settling onto the floor, rolling a canopic jar made in the figure of a mummified man with the head of a jackal under a nearby table, out of the way. Tuamutef, son of Horus, he thought absently. Tuamutef and his brothers were the guardians of the parts of the body of the dead; this particular jar would contain the stomach of the deceased. The goddess Neith was Tuamutef's protector. She wasn't going to be happy about having her protégé knocked around like that.

The owner of the stomach probably wouldn't

be too happy about it either, come to think of it. He wondered where the other jars were, the ones that held the mummy's lungs, liver, and intestines. Probably lying around somewhere, but at the moment he had a more compelling interest to follow.

Inside, a wooden coffin, this one painted and lined with hieroglyphs, with carved channels filled with molten gold to outline them. He didn't bother to translate them, but lifted away that lid too, too eager now to see what lay beneath. All around him, the walls were crowded with the figures of the Egyptian gods, the tale of the Book of the Dead, of Coming Forth By Day, the script and ritual by which the ancient Egyptians passed through the portal of death into the afterlife.

The coffin contained, of course, a mummy wrapped in linen, its shape vaguely suggestive of the arms crossed across its chest, the details of its appearance completely obliterated by the layers upon layers of protective wrappings. Unlike all the rest of the mummies he had found through the years, this one looked as if it had been laid to rest only yesterday, the strips of linen faintly discolored from the natron used to dry out the body but still flexible, not stiff with age. As he reached out to touch the featureless head, he felt something tugging at his ankle. He looked down.

It was a jackal—a wooden jackal, alive somehow. A black jackal wearing a broad collar of gold and faience, studded with red and blue gems. Its black eyes sparkled at him. Its ears were huge. So were its jaws.

Anubis. Anubis, with tail wagging, snuffling at his shoe, his gorgeous faience collar still a part of his body. Anubis, god and guardian of the underworld—inspecting him.

He jerked his foot away, and the wooden jackal sat back and looked up at him. The powerful jaws opened, and a wooden tongue lolled out from between glossy ivory teeth as Anubis panted happily at him, his black eyes twinkling, his short wooden tail clacking against the stone floor. One paw reached up, past his waist, to his shoulder, rested there as if claiming him. He was eye to eye with the god.

There was no place to go. The wooden figure was three times the size of a mortal jackal, its jaws appropriately massive. He was backed against the edge of the golden sarcophagus. He looked around wildly for some way to escape.

The mummy sat up, turned its head toward him, blindly studying him. Eyes opened in the wrappings, stared at him.

On its linen-wrapped shoulders gleamed the brass stars of a general.

Behold, the Osiris Hammond shall come forth by day to perform everything he desires upon the earth among the living, ran the hieroglyphic script along the rim of the coffin.

Enough of this! came the frustrated cry of the Kayeechi council to Etra'ain. *Shape within the shape! If you cannot find what we seek, we will find it for you!*

CHAPTER SEVEN

Water moved against Jack O'Neill's skin like cool silk, moved in and out of his lungs like a caress. He breathed deeply of it, sighed, and swam onward toward the reef. He'd dived often among the great reefs of the world, and wished that he could dispense with the encumbrance of aqualung and flippers. Now, it seemed, he'd succeeded. He was breathing the water as easily as any of the fish he swam with.

The reef was a mass of twists and towers, blues and greens and reds and golds. Eels hid in coral caves, dashed out to seize their prey. Thousands of fish with rainbow-hued, shimmering fins surrounded him, nibbling curiously, then swerved away, as disciplined as a military drill team, heading for a more palatable source of food. He could almost hear them rejecting his flavor as too much of the world above the surface.

O'Neill paused, treading water, and looked down at a continent of sea life, spreading as far as his eyes could see. Transparent jellyfish, thousands of venomous tentacles dangling, glided slowly by beneath him. Sharks cruised, looking for blood. An entire cycle of life—predators, prey, scavengers, parasites, and symbiotes—was spread out before him, moving in a perfect, silent ecosystem. None of them looked up; none of them took note of the water-breathing human intruder who had invaded their universe. He had gone diving in Australia, at the Great Barrier Reef, in the Caribbean and the Mediterranean. It was one of his favorite things to do on leave, one of the most relaxing things he could think of. Nowhere, though, had he felt as much a part of the life of the sea as he did here.

And there beside him swam an octopus with an odd pattern of auburn fur on its head and along its tentacles, reaching out to him with one graceful arm, the tip encircling his wrist, tugging at him for attention. He turned to look at it and noted without surprise that the eyes that blinked back were Vair's. Somehow it seemed natural and appropriate that his acquaintance from P4V-837 should accompany him here.

More than company, he soon realized, Vair was acting as a guide. He showed O'Neill over the reef, introducing him to the manta rays buried in the sand, which when disturbed flapped their way free like underwater birds. He pointed out the delicate flowerlike growths of fan coral. The two of them chased schools of vivid red and gold fingerlings and were chased in turn when the school changed its direction and pursued them instead. They played tag with sharks, and O'Neill rubbed his fingertips along the sandpaper skin and stared directly into the expressionless black eyes and down the gullets encircled by rows of teeth. When the shark turned toward him he kicked away, and the animal forgot him immediately, seeking more apt prey.

He was laughing at his own daring when the octopus directed his attention to a distant part of the coral reef. When it was satisfied that he was looking in the right direction, it gathered its multiple limbs together and shot away, leading him. He followed, curious, willing to see what new surprises the reef held.

Mostly, the coral below him still swarmed with life, but as he followed Vair, he noticed longer and longer stretches where the color had leached out of the living rock, where the coral had died, leaving only ghost-white skeletons behind. He paused to study one such area, and the Vair-octopus paused with him, floating patiently, maintaining its place in the cool current with tiny movements of its tentacles.

The coral wall was shattered, with huge gaping holes, as if something had exploded within it or physically ripped it apart. Pieces still floated and settled to the white sand of the ocean floor. The ubiquitous schools of fish kept away, and the predators that fed on them avoided the ruins as well. He kicked his way down to touch the damaged reef, only to find that even in death the coral was razor sharp, and his fingers came away bleeding.

Sharks could smell blood in the water from miles away. He looked around quickly, his hair waving in the water much like the jellyfish tentacles, but even the sharks avoided these ruins.

Vair-octopus sank down beside him and reached out again, touching his bleeding hand with the tip of a tentacle. There were no suckers on the alien's aquatic form, he noticed, and as he thought the thought, the grayish circular pads appeared in neat twin rows from tip to body.

Vair led him onward, past more sections of the reef living and dead. As he swam, O'Neill began to realize that he could hear something.

At first it was only the pressure of deep water against his eardrums, thrumming. Then he heard a distinct snap as a shark flashed by to sink its teeth into the side of a manatee, followed by a thin, gurgling scream as the mammal was dragged into the depths. A dozen more sharks circled and dove, and the screaming stopped as thin red tendrils rose upward through the water. He could taste the blood in his mouth, in his lungs, and he swam faster to get away from the tainted liquid. The sharks lashed by, ignoring him.

And then he could hear a dull, crumbling roar somewhere ahead of them. Vair was leading him toward the source of the sound, angling upward to give him a broader perspective.

From the height, he could see the end of the massive reef, stopping clifflike while the sea floor spread out endlessly beyond it.

Gathered at one blue-and-gold tower, swarming over its surface, were hundreds of octopi, their multiple limbs wrapped around the coral, their beaks chopping and tearing holes in the living rock. As the pieces of reef were torn away, they lost their color and drifted to the seafloor, lifeless and white. The roar was coming from the crumbling of the coral towers.

He looked over at Vair in dismay. Vair blinked and waved his attention back to the destruction.

Yes, octopi, but *different*. Not Kayeechi. As if "octopi" stood for "live things," but not the Kayeechi, even if Vair took their form.

No. That couldn't be right either, because

somehow he knew that the stone of the coral itself was alive, just as the sea life—the fish and anemones and men o'war that inhabited the reef were alive.

The coral fought back, its inhabitants massing over one or another of the attackers, and sometimes one of the not-Kayeechi octopi would go tumbling down to the sea floor too, where giant rays would rise up and snatch them out of the helpless descent and tear them to pieces. As he watched he could see the defending rays going from one multiarmed target to the next, methodically.

As they did so, the octopi would fall back, regroup, and choose another, weaker point to rip through the coral walls.

They were intelligent, he realized. Both sides were intelligent, and he was watching a pitched battle of deadly enemies.

Vair touched his arm again, bringing his attention to the submachine gun he hadn't been carrying until now. He brought it up slowly against the resistance of the water, then allowed the bore to drift downward to aim at empty sand. In this place, the weapon was useless. He didn't know how to tell Vair that, or even which side he was supposed to fire upon.

Vair pushed at the weapon, urging him to use it, waving with other tentacles at the battle. He shook his head. Vair pushed again, then shot off to the battle, diving into the middle of it, entangling himself with one of the rival octopi.

O'Neill couldn't tell them apart. The water roiled, and he could barely see the multiple limbs thrashing at one another, much less be able to tell what belonged to whom.

Does he not see? What would it take for him to use the weapon?

Perhaps it requires a direct threat to his own welfare.

Very well. We can provide that.

He was still trying to focus on Vair versus not Vair when something stabbed him in the right calf. He doubled over to see a moray eel easily as long as he was tall lock its jaws in the muscle below and behind the knee, shaking its head back and forth to tear a chunk of flesh free. There was no pain yet, only the thrashing of the hungry eel and the spreading cloud of blood. Vair, beside him again, apparently undamaged from his own battle, kept pushing at the gun, urging him to use it.

He had nothing to lose but a moray mouthful of gastrocnemius. Raising the submachine gun, he pulled the trigger.

As a live-fire demonstration, it was a complete failure. As a deterrent to the eel, it was also a complete failure. Four or five bullets flashed through the water in slow motion, and then the weapon jammed. He reversed it and pounded at the massive jaws. The eel let go and backed away, the better to rush him and attack again.

He pulled great gulps of water into his lungs, seeking more oxygen, more fuel for his effort. The injured leg was hampering his attempts to remain oriented toward the eel, which somehow seemed much larger now. It opened its jaws impossibly wide, unhinging them so that they made a nearly perfect oval of incredibly sharp teeth, and shot toward him as if the pressure of the water was insignificant.

Vair floated politely in the water nearby, observing.

The moray started to close its jaws just a little too early. He had twisted back but was unable to avoid the rush; his flailing attempts to get clear had only landed his arm into the animal's mouth. The fangs left long, oozing scratches along his biceps when he yanked himself away.

The action caught the eel by surprise, and he shoved the submachine gun into its mouth crosswise. For a fleeting instant he imagined pointing the weapon down its throat and blowing the eel's minuscule brains out, but the gun was too waterlogged to fire.

The jaws clamped shut, or as nearly shut as they could get, considering the amount of steel they were struggling to cut through. He used the butt as a pivot point and swung himself in slow motion above and behind the eel, or as much above and behind a slender, three-dimensionally writhing and very angry fish as he could get, locking both hands around the eel's head to hold the gun in place. The eel's teeth were easily six inches long, and he tried to get the barrel behind them, where the joint of the jaw should be but wasn't, judging by how wide that mouth was gaping. At least with the gun in its mouth the eel couldn't take another bite out of *him*.

He was trying to ride the thing like a scaly bucking bronco, and it was a supremely useless effort. He could feel the barrel sliding along its teeth and had to pull frantically to keep his hand from sliding right along with it. The screeching, scraping sound hurt his ears. The rest of the eel's body thrashed against his—a long, flat panel of solid muscle, impossible to keep hold of, impossible to hang on to. He was beginning to tire. His leg was numb and useless. The eel jerked again, bringing his face down next to its, and for an instant he was looking it directly in the eye.

The fish couldn't blink. He'd be damned if he would either.

An instant later he was getting an excellent view of its fang-fringed gullet as it attempted to open its jaws and spit the gun out, flipping him in the process over its head. He jammed the barrel back as far as he could, but the animal had twisted away from him again and his action was pushing the creature away instead of pulling the choke deeper into place. All it would take would be for the eel to continue backing away, and he would *have* to let go. With one leg essentially useless, he couldn't possibly keep up with it.

No sooner thought than done, and the eel was out of reach and shaking the useless gun away. It took two tries, because the fangs got caught in the trigger guard. The last he saw of the weapon was a glint of silver as it went spinning into a cemetery of coral, breaking down yet more of the brittle dead reef. The infuriated eel gathered itself for a final charge.

Ever helpful, Vair waved tentacles frantically, directing his attention away from the charging eel to yet another threat.

A flotilla of sharks had risen in the water in the near distance—an odd mixture of hammerheads and blues and great whites and nurse sharks, species that didn't belong together and certainly wouldn't engage in feeding frenzy together. It didn't seem to matter; they were all being drawn by the irresistible smell of blood in the water. His blood.

And the eel was almost on top of him.

He needed to get out of there, but he was a

water breather now too. Where would he be safe? Not on the surface. Certainly not here, out of his element. He needed—

A weapon. The thoughts were warm with eager satisfaction.

Then the man they observed shaped and released his response to the sharks, and a cloud of dark green, smelly ink discolored the water around him. The eel took the first impact and thrashed frantically, shaking its grip on the human loose, flinging itself away, knocking the human into Kayeechi and then convulsing wildly until finally it went limp and sank to the floor of the sea, its black eyes as expressionless in death as in life.

The first of the sharks encountered the farthest edge of the green and shook itself wildly, trying to back out of the cloud.

Seeing the erratic swimming pattern, the other sharks turned on the first one. This lasted only until they, too, got a whiff of the green-dyed water, at which they doubled back on themselves in their attempt to flee.

The observers were bewildered.

What is it? What has he done?

O'Neill floated in place and watched as the sharks, and every other finned thing, left the area in indecent haste. This repellant stuff seemed to work better here than it ever had before; not even the growing red mist in the water kept their interest. Once they tasted the green ink, they fled.

Considering the taste of the stuff, he couldn't blame them. He'd met skunks that— Well, that was an insult to the skunk clan. The stench was unbearable. For a scent hunter like an eel or a shark, it would have been like being hit with a lightning bolt. For the moray, maybe that had been the truth.

Finally only Vair and he were left, and the auburn octopus looked as if it would very much like to leave too. His injured leg was beginning to hurt now. He twisted around in the water to examine the gashes left by the moray's fangs.

Why are we wasting time this way? Why did you return to this one?

Be still! I am the One who Shapes, and I tell you that there are potent weapons here in this man. Did you see what he did? He has a mist that can drive his enemies away!

Yes, a mist under water! We are not water breathers! We need what we can use here! *Why do you permit him to continue this scenario?*

Unwilling admission: *My control of these aliens is not strong. I do not understand them or the nature of all the weapons or even the places we see. They come out of the Nothing; they are not water breathers either. I do not know how or why or what would shape this. It is a struggle to control them—you saw it yourself when you walked in his dream.*

Swam *in it, you mean.* The thoughts were contemptuous. *Eha, what kind of person swims? What kind of person swims so deep? The surface of the water was far over his head!*

A ripple of shock spread around the little circle, as if contempt were something utterly new to them. The gathered Kayeechi looked at each other uncertainly, uncomfortably, except for Vair, who stood dripping wet and angry, facing the leader of the little group. A green miasma clung faintly to his fur pattern. The others tried to edge away without being too obvious about it.

Swam, then, Etra'ain responded at last. *My point remains. I cannot control them too closely, or we lose the benefit of their dreams. We seek what they have, not what we permit them to have; we must take what we can from them. We must let them create the context of the dream, even if it is underwater, to find new things. This mist he used—perhaps we should consider using some kind of green water smoke to repel the Narrai.*

And perhaps it would work if the Narrai, or we, were water creatures! In any case I tell you that a mere repellant will not be enough. We are running out of time. If the Narrai return before we are ready, they will destroy us completely. The sun rises and we are counting our dead. We must destroy them first. I tell you, Etra'ain, seek another dream, another shape!

CHAPTER EIGHT

Etra'ain sat alone in the Circle of Shaping and watched the sun rise over the hills where the Narrai nested. Ever since their Shapers had dreamed the giant birds and walking trees, the hills had been the home of the great birds.

It had seemed so easy to begin with, shaping their dreams, the dreams of others, even the dreams of the little creatures of the earth and sky. Over time, over generations, the Shaped dreams became real and stayed real even when the dreamers woke and so built many different shapes to their world.

How were the Kayeechi of long ago to know that the Narrai would eventually pull free of the dreams, would not submit to the Shaping of later generations, would learn so quickly, fight back so devastatingly? How were they to know that the great birds would one day refuse to submit to having their nests plundered to feed the young of their creators? The tide of war had turned against the Kayeechi, and now it was a matter of survival.

And now she was driven to seek the dreams of these aliens who had weapons, she was sure, beyond any of those she had Shaped before. Greater even than these.

She reached out with a withered three-fingered hand to touch the smooth metal of an energy staff. She was not certain it would work, because she was not certain how it functioned, but she had seen in the dreams that the dark one was comfortable and familiar with it, and she had shaped it whole from his mind. Vair would have to take it to the dark one and see if he recognized it and would put the seal of reality upon it.

It was not the weapon Vair sought, but if the staff worked, it would help immeasurably.

Meanwhile, she was not finished mining the dreams of the aliens. They would win yet, if she had to Shape the future itself, which would be the greatest Shaping of all.

"Mmmmmmm." There was nothing, *nothing* like the warm, slightly scratchy feel of clean beach sand against bare skin, the soothing sound of surf washing against the shore in lazy, endless repetition. Samantha Carter squinted into the brilliant blue overhead, and the brief shadow of a gull shaded her eyes.

Behind her was a tropical forest climbing all the way to the top of a round hill. In the forest, she could find gorgeous birds and exotic fruits ripe for the taking. She was absolutely alone on the island. She could sun herself naked and no one would know or care. She was at perfect peace except, perhaps, for the heat of the sun against her face. It was like being on another world, where she didn't have to worry about the military or secrets or Stargates or enemy aliens or even getting to work on time. She could just lie here, laze and doze, forever and ever and ever. It was pure bliss.

Was this her memory, she wondered, or Jolinar's? Her beaches were usually crowded with tourists, and she lay on a towel or a chaise longue with an umbrella-topped drink beside her. A major's pay and a major's leave rarely ran to tropical paradises. Jolinar's might, though. The Goa'uld's memories were not something she normally sought out, but if this were one of them, she was happy to luxuriate in it. There had to be some kind of upside to the experience, after all.

And she supposed even Tok'ra, even Goa'uld, occasionally went on vacation.

God, that sun felt good.

Etra'ain let herself slide through the shaping, observing the alien mind. It had an odd double quality to it, something like that the dark one had as well. It made it more difficult to propose scenarios to the dreaming minds. Memories, even partial ones, were even more difficult to call forth from this one; it was almost as if she were dealing with two adult minds in one. She wondered how these strange, tall beings remained sane with all the clutter they retained. It was, though she would admit it to no one and particularly not to Vair or Shasee, completely overwhelming sometimes.

But there had to be a key in their minds too. She was the Shaper; she refused to admit that there was any dream, no matter how alien, how bizarre, she could not access and make real.

Except, perhaps, her own hollow dreams of victory.

But that was not at issue here. She would look again, and this time she would find something useful.

A tiny scratching sound off to Samantha's left called her attention. It was a red—no, a deep purple crab, perhaps half as large as the palm of her hand, waving its larger claw up in the air as if trying to attract her attention. Tiny spines grew out of its chitin in a regular crosshatch pattern.

"Hi there," she responded, amused. "Looking

for a new home? There's lots of real estate out here. I'll share."

The crab took two steps sideways, then skittered in the opposite direction, still maintaining a careful distance from its human observer. Its antennae wavered back and forth at the sound of her voice. The little crustacean's attitude reminded her of a teenage boy on a stag line, trying to work up his courage to dash across the breadth of the auditorium and ask one of the girls to dance.

"Hey, I don't bite," she said.

The crab waved its larger claw at her again. It was a very big claw for a little crab. Very businesslike.

"And you're not going to bite either, are you?" she asked, feeling mild alarm.

Suddenly the claw came down again, and the little crab zipped backward. "Hey," she protested, lifting herself up on one elbow to watch as it disappeared under a pile of brown seaweed.

The waves slapping against the shore were suddenly cold against her legs, and she twisted around to see a series of much larger waves moving in. A maelstrom a few hundred yards out sent seabirds screeching away.

Instead of sinking down into the water, the whirlpool moved up into the air, as if something were pushing the water out rather than pulling it in. Now really alarmed, she rose to one knee, watching as the whirlpool moved closer.

And then a massive, dull white, bulbous head broke out of the whirlpool, with two gigantic brown eyes that blinked and watched impassively as multiple arms flailed, picking a stray gull out of the air and flinging it to land broken at her feet. It was something out of a childhood movie—*20,000 Leagues Under the Sea*—but there was no Jules Verne to write her ending for her.

But for no apparent reason, there were weapons on the sand beside her, set out in a neat array. Without taking time to choose, she grabbed a zatnickatel and sighted along it as the kraken splashed closer, supporting itself on its multiple arms, its beak clacking. The thing could have heaved a small submarine at her.

She was sorry to have thought it as a misty cigar shape began to coalesce within the kraken's tentacles. The weapons beside her were now piled recklessly together. She could see a combat knife, a fighting staff, a bow with arrows. Or was the quarterstaff really an energy staff? And was that a jumble of ribbons made to wrap around a Goa'uld hand?

Never mind. She already had a weapon to hand, and the kraken was thrashing closer. She had to crane her head back to see it.

It didn't frighten her. She never panicked in

combat. Afterward, in the privacy of her own quarters, she might allow herself five minutes to shake like a leaf, cry, wonder how in the hell she'd survived when so many others in her circumstances hadn't. But when it mattered, she kept her head and did what had to be done. It was something she was proud of, and it was a huge factor in her getting as far as she had in the Air Force.

So no damned nightmare out of nineteenth-century "scientifiction" was going to take her down now. Especially not when she was on vacation.

She fired—once, twice, three times. The brown eyes blinked in outright shock as a significant part of the kraken's white head evaporated. In one of those frozen moments that seemed to last forever and never really did, she could see the sky and part of a cloud in the semicircular gap that took the place of its cranium. It hovered in place just long enough for her to raise the gun again, and then the thing toppled back into the sea with a mighty splash.

The impact triggered a larger wave, one that grew and grew and grew, towering over her. Overwhelming her. The curling rim of the wave was white with froth and spume, but unlike any other wave she had ever seen before, this one did not fall into itself.

It became a mountain, higher than Everest, the white wave rim solidifying and soaring white-capped into the clouds, its steep slopes rising from right in front of her to the skies above. What the sunlight lost in warmth it gained in brightness as it reflected off fields of snow dotted here and there with lonely outcrops of rock. She was no longer nude, but fully dressed in winter gear, and observing the mountain openmouthed through snow goggles and a rim of frost-repellent fur around the hood of her parka.

As she watched, thunder rumbled in the clear sky, and a massive sheet of snow cracked loose from the summit and hung in space for a para-lyzing moment before roaring down at her. She flung the useless zat gun away and turned to run just as the avalanche reached her. For some rea-son the tropical island, complete with palm trees and sand and brightly colored birds and dead volcano cone, was still there, and she was run-ning in place on the beach sand, her arctic boots digging in deep but taking her nowhere. At her feet, as she ran in place, she could see the crab rooting around in the pile of weapons, as if look-ing for a new shelter. She could feel the wall of snow thundering closer and closer.

She woke shaking, jerking her head around to find the threatening snowmass. It wasn't there.

Nor was the beach, or the palm trees, or the

parrots. Jimmy Buffett had definitely left the building.

She was in a small cave, lying near one wall. A few feet away, Daniel Jackson sprawled, muttering to himself as he slept. Teal'C slept on his back, as if at attention, and if anything, his habitual frown was engraved even deeper in his features. Closest to the entrance lay Jack O'Neill, prone and in the act of rolling over, flinging one arm as if to push someone or something away.

The sky outside was light. Sunrise was long past. Why wasn't someone already awake, watching? What had happened to their defensive perimeter?

"Colonel O'Neill?" she called quietly, getting to her feet but keeping clear of her superior officer's reach. "Sir?"

O'Neill mumbled, but failed to wake up completely.

She edged along the wall of the cave to check outside. The open patch of grass appeared empty and harmless. She could see easily through the scattered trees. A faint path led through them and out of sight. It too was empty.

She could hear the wind and birds and insects. The ever present fragrance of incense was hardly noticeable anymore; she had to concentrate to really smell it.

There were no suspicious solid patches in the

boughs of the trees—patches that might turn out to be enemy snipers.

And despite what Daniel had said, there were absolutely no buildings in sight. Period.

Of course, she couldn't see any frame, stucco, or brick houses either, but she didn't really expect to. They'd left the town behind them when they were led to the cave for their second campsite. It was an isolated spot, deliberately chosen to be, she was sure. A sort of Kayeechi quarantine, in fact. It made sense to keep strangers far away until you were certain of their intentions.

Taking a deep breath, she decided that, as long as she was up, she'd better find the designated bush. There might not be time later, and besides, if the others woke up, the designated bush might turn out to be a roomful of windows. Too many things had a habit of changing abruptly around here.

Finishing without incident, she faded back into the cave, chose a small rock, and tossed it at her commanding officer from a safe distance.

O'Neill muttered angrily and shifted onto his back, shaking his head. Even in his sleep, he was feeling around for his rifle. He definitely wasn't getting a lot of rest.

None of them were, she was willing to bet. She still felt tired, as if she really had run in sand while wearing a full arctic pack. It would be good to get back home and sleep in her own bed for a while.

"Colonel? Colonel!"

After a moment, O'Neill's eyes snapped open. Even in the vague light near the back of the cave, she could see the resemblance between his sharp brown eyes and those of the kraken in her dream. Was her subconscious trying to tell her that her commander was a giant octopus with tentacles? And what exactly was he supposed to be using those tentacles for? She bit her lip hard to stifle her response to that image. *Literally*, she snickered, *in my dreams!*

But where had the avalanche come from? Was it one of Jolinar's memories? Or was it an obscure Freudian message from the back of her brain that things were out of control, that she was feeling overwhelmed by events?

And why? She'd handled the kraken without much difficulty.

While she was mulling it over, O'Neill's long body contracted, and when it straightened again, he was on his feet. The humor of the moment was gone. "Carter? What's going on?"

"I don't know, sir. I was sleeping, and when I woke up—"

"Is there a problem?" It was Teal'C, sitting up. Characteristically, there didn't seem to be any in-between drowsiness for the Jaffa; one moment he was sound asleep and the next wide-awake. It was a knack Carter wished she shared sometimes. It always took a major jolt of adrenaline for her to wake up that completely, and a jolt like that was never a good sign for how the day was going to go.

Between them, Jackson continued to mutter in his sleep. The two little lines between his eyebrows that meant he was thinking hard about something were deep and longer than usual. Carter stepped closer to hear what he was saying, but it was in ancient Egyptian. She hoped he was talking to Sha're. She knew how much he missed his late wife. It would be nice if he could see her again, if only in his dreams.

But that wasn't the issue right now. "Who's on watch?" she asked, turning back to the others. The three of them looked at each other.

"I was," O'Neill said slowly, running his hand through his hair. "I was, and I must have fallen asleep before I woke anyone else up."

Carter blinked. Not that she would have expected any of them to fall asleep on watch, but . . . "That's bizarre." She moved past O'Neill to look out the mouth of the cave again. Nothing had changed in the past five minutes. "That's not the kind of thing you *do*, sir."

"I should hope the hell not." He got up and

looked over his weapons and their packs. "Is anything missing?"

Teal'C immediately started sorting through the packs. Next to him, Carter did the same thing, shoving one of Daniel's arms out of the way to reach his. The archaeologist continued to mutter, now with a somewhat more aggrieved tone, but he did not wake up.

"Everything appears to be as it was," Teal'C reported at last. Carter nodded in confirmation. "Is it possible that we were somehow drugged?"

"The food?" Carter suggested. "But you didn't eat anything, sir."

He shook his head, angrily. "Not true. The little silver guy showed up with some more apples after you were all asleep. Dammit, I knew better!"

"If you were drugged, then so were we all," the Jaffa reminded him. "And as I said, everything appears to be as it was. Nothing is missing or disturbed."

"That's unusual all by itself." The colonel took a deep breath, considering. "Hell. Maybe we *were* all drugged for some reason. I think I like that better than the thought that I fell asleep on watch."

"It is very serious," Teal'C remarked, "but in this case no harm seems to have been done."

O'Neill gave the Jaffa a wry smile. "That

makes it *perfectly* okay then," he said in a tone that said clearly it was anything but. He moved to join Carter at the mouth of the cave. "All right, Major, what do *you* see out there?"

"Trees, sir. A park, maybe, or a forest. There's a footpath—I think the way we came up here last night."

"So far, so good. Teal'C?"

"Yes. I also see trees." He paused. "And a small, gray-striped animal eating grass at the base of the largest one." He paused again. "The animal has gone away."

"Somebody wake up Daniel. I want to know if it's unanimous. And if it changes, speak up."

Teal'C nudged the archaeologist, and with a startled snort Jackson finally woke up. "Huh?"

"Up and at 'em, Daniel."

"Huh?" Jackson fumbled for his glasses and stared blearily through them at the others, looked around and shuddered convulsively. "God, what a dream!"

"I'll see your dream and raise you a nightmare," O'Neill snapped. "Come on. I want you to look out here and tell me what you see."

Still groggy but amenable, Jackson heaved himself to his feet and peered out the mouth of the cave. After a moment he removed his specs, rubbed his eyes, smothered a yawn, and put on his glasses again.

"I see trees," he stated definitively. "Many, many trees. And a path. So what?"

O'Neill took a deep breath. "I'm not sure what. So far we've got cute little aliens, some wildly different perceptions of this world, and me falling asleep on watch."

"And bad dreams," Teal'C added.

"And bad dreams," O'Neill agreed. "So what does that add up to?"

"Uh, not much?" Jackson asked, yawning.

"I *don't* fall asleep on watch, Daniel."

"Well, you're not perfect either, Jack. Look, it's a new world. Maybe you're allergic to something here. Antihistamines always make me sleepy. Maybe the smoke, or the food, or something else in the air, or all three just had that effect on you. Nobody's hurt, right? Nobody's been captured or tortured or—" At the look on O'Neill's face, Jackson shut up.

"Some of the aliens are coming," Teal'C reported. "I see the silver one."

"And isn't that Eleb?" Carter asked, glad to help change the subject.

The two little aliens, brown and silver, were indeed moving quickly up the path toward them, dodging between the trees but making no attempt to hide. A moment's consultation indicated that all four of them saw the same thing:

short aliens, concensus on fur color, same number of fingers—three—on each small hand . . . .

"But wait a minute," Carter said as Eleb got closer. "What's that they're carrying?"

Daniel rubbed his eyes and looked again, just to be sure, as the Kayeechi caught sight of all of them gathered in the mouth of the cave. The Kayeechi waved to them merrily. "How the heck did they get their hands on a zat gun?"

CHAPTER NINE

"I don't care how," O'Neill snapped. "On alert."
He paused, then amended, "Yeah, I do care. We
didn't bring any zats with us, did we? We're not
missing any?"

"We did not bring them this time," Teal'C confirmed. While the zatnickatel, a Goa'uld weapon,
was usually a standard part of their armory, their
availability was limited while Earth scientists
continued to try to figure out how the damn
things worked. This time they had relied on standard military issue, except, of course, for Teal'C's
energy staff. "And all of our weaponry is present
and accounted for."

The members of the team not already on their
feet rose and scrambled for their weapons, trying
hard to behave as if this was the casual and normal way that a Terran exploratory team got up
every morning, as the Kayeechi came up the
path to the mouth of the cave. The aliens weren't

making any threatening gestures; they were simply armed with weapons that, by all accounts, they shouldn't have. And by the way they were holding the things, perhaps "armed" wasn't the best choice of words either. They didn't seem completely clear on the distinction between barrel and butt.

"Welcome, welcome, morning greetings," Shasee chirped as he came up to them, holding the Goa'uld weapon awkwardly in his three-fingered hands. The silver-furred one looked tired, a rim of red around his copper-colored eyes. Elbe was moving slowly, favoring one leg. "Did you dream well? Was your sleep good to you?"

"Not exactly," O'Neill growled.

Jackson, as team anthropologist, stepped in. "Uh, well, pretty good. You look tired. Did *you* dream well?"

The two aliens didn't appear to comprehend his attempt to return what looked like a ritual greeting. "We wish to welcome our guests on this new day," Elbe said.

"Well, er, thank you," Jackson said lamely.

Impatient of the courtesies, O'Neill cut to the chase. "What's that you've got there, Shasee? Elbe? And where'd you get them?"

The aliens twisted their faces in a version of a smile and stepped up to Carter. The team tensed; O'Neill had his sidearm half out of its holster.

But the aliens merely held the zat guns out to her. "Please see," they said. "Is it perfect?"

Carter took the weapons cautiously, and the rest of the team exhaled and relaxed minutely. Carter tucked one into her belt and turned the other one over in her hands, examining it from every angle, and then she looked first at O'Neill, and then at the alien. "Yes," she agreed. "It's perfect. Where did you get it, Shasee?"

Shasee tittered and held out his hand for the gun. When Carter made no indication that she was inclined to give it back, he exchanged a worried glance with his companion. "Please?" he asked. "It is perfect? It works? Please return it."

"Well, it *looks* perfect," Carter temporized. "I don't know whether it *works* or not. I'd have to test fire it and . . . stuff."

"There are more Kayeechi coming," Teal'C reported from the crest of the little hill. "And they have—they appear to have—an energy staff."

It was true. Four more of the little Kayeechi were coming up the path. Two were carrying the ubiquitous braziers dangling on chains, with threads of nearly colorless smoke flavoring the air. Another had armfuls of new-looking baskets heaped with fruit and bread, while yet another was lugging several large flasks. The last was hefting a Jaffa energy staff, dragging it by the wrong end and catching it on the bushes as he came. Fortunately it wasn't entirely easy to trigger an energy staff unless you happened to know what you were doing, but the careless way the little guy handled the thing made it clear that he had absolutely no idea of the extent of the destructive power of the weapon.

"What the *hell* is going on?" O'Neill asked. His team, recognizing a rhetorical question when they heard one, wisely did not attempt to answer.

Puffing, the alien finally made it to the group and promptly offered its burden to Teal'C for review.

Teal'C accepted the staff and examined it. He kept his own staff close at hand, with his body between it and the assembled Kayeechi, who were trying to get a good look up close.

"It appears to be a fully functioning weapon," Teal'C said. With a glance at O'Neill, he triggered it, and the bulbous firing end separated into four distinct leaves surrounding a core of energy.

"Fire it please," the alien who had dragged it up the hill said. It—it wasn't clear, from close up, whether the little one was male, female, or something else entirely—was watching Teal'C's every move intently.

"Where did you find this?" Teal'C asked gruffly. His imposing glare had no impact, for once. The little alien, whose fur was a delicate rose pink, merely watched the dark, capable hands curled comfortably around the shaft as if it might miss something vital if it removed its gaze.

"These things are ours," Shasee answered instead. He was still holding out his hand to Carter, waiting for her to return the zat gun. "They are like yours, but they belong to us."

"How do you know they're like ours?" O'Neill asked. "I mean, that staff looks like Teal'C's, sure. But these other things? We don't carry anything like that."

Shasee closed his eyes and took a deep breath, as if he would rather be doing almost anything than arguing with this bizarre visitor to his people. "Car Ter said that this was perfect, so she must be familiar with it."

"Yes," Daniel said, "but are *you* familiar with these things? Do you know what they can do?"

"Show us," the rose-colored alien piped up.

O'Neill sighed. It was difficult to get past the perception that these small, downright *cute* beings were children, clamoring to play with dangerous weapons, but it was obvious from their demeanor, both the night before and now, that they were not. He didn't want to introduce any snakes into Eden, but the snakes were already there. If the aliens had found a storehouse of

Goa'uld weapons, it was better that they know how to use them than they should find out by accident. He shuddered, remembering Charlie with an ache that would never completely go away.

Not only that, but if the Goa'uld or their Jaffa slaves had a store of weapons on this world, it changed his own plans considerably. He needed to know more, and the easiest way to get the information would be to cooperate with the natives. And if he could make a deal with them for those weapons, so much the better.

"Teal'C, were the Jaffa in the habit of stashing away weapons and supplies on worlds they weren't visiting much?"

"No," the Jaffa answered. "Not while I was First Prime. It would be considered wasteful. Also, it would be seen as a lack of faith in our Goa'uld masters, who supplied us with whatever we needed."

"The Tok'ra?" Carter suggested cautiously. "Might they have been here?"

"You tell us," O'Neill said. "You're the one with Jolinar's memories."

Carter shook her head. "Not that easily, sir. And even if she didn't know about it, doesn't mean they don't do it."

"The weapons had to have come from somewhere," Jackson pointed out, "because here they *are*."

"Yeah. Here they are. Go ahead, Teal'C," O'Neill said harshly. "Show them what it can do."

Teal'C raised the staff to his shoulder in one smooth movement and fired. The rose alien was still watching him, and so missed the sight of a large boulder being blown to splinters behind him.

The rest of the aliens, however, including Shasee and Elbe, did not. There was a shocked silence in response to the explosion, and then another of the aliens cried out something the team didn't understand.

The rest of the crowd, however, did, and they converged on Teal'C, allowing him a circle of free space to move within but jammed together, separated from him by an invisible barrier of personal space. With O'Neill's assent, the former Jaffa First demonstrated how the triggering mechanism worked and how the staff was fired. He was a little more reluctant to let the rose alien try, however, particularly when the little one had to struggle to balance the long staff in its short arms. Even Shasee was drawn away from Carter long enough to make an attempt, but the staff was simply too long and too awkward.

The zat gun, however, while still large for most hands, was far easier to handle. That made it more accessible to the Kayeechi—and made O'Neill correspondingly more uneasy.

"Look," he said. "If you fire this at someone and it hits, the first time it will hurt them. Badly. The second time they die.

"The third time, they disappear. It is not a toy, it is not a joke. It is a weapon, a terrible weapon."

"Yes," Shasee agreed. "Very terrible. Show us."

For all the warnings, the Kayeechi didn't seem to really understand the power they were dealing with. Despite their misgivings, however, the team showed the Kayeechi how the zat gun operated. The aliens were delighted and lined up eagerly to try it out. Several trees disappeared as a result.

By the time everyone had had an opportunity to try the zat gun, Elbe had organized the food into another picnic feast, this time without the canopy. The ubiquitous incense burners were set in place and lit. Roughly woven cloth was laid out as if for a picnic, and the food and bread and wine were laid out and SG-1 invited to partake. The weariness that had characterized all the Kayeechi on their arrival had evaporated, and they were chattering to each other eagerly, passing the zat gun around. At least, O'Neill noted, they kept it pointed to the ground; humans unaccustomed to such things would have inevitably pointed them at each other. He could only hope that the repeated practice had used up the charge.

"Come and feast with us!" Elbe invited them as the small party of visitors sat on the ground around the impromptu picnic rug and looked up expectantly. The energy staff and zat guns had been set, almost reverently, in the middle of the feast.

Jackson, Carter, and Teal'C all looked at O'Neill.

"In the middle of shooting up the landscape, I don't suppose anyone happened to let it slip where they got these things," the colonel asked. Even though it was obvious that *this* question was anything but rhetorical, no one ventured an answer.

"I still think we ought to pack up and haul out of here," he added. He had an uneasy feeling he'd said that before.

"We really need to find out how these people manage to change our perceptions," Daniel objected mildly. He had bread in his hand, he tore off a piece and ate it. When O'Neill raised an eyebrow, the archaeologist shrugged. "Hey, it's breakfast. It's not bad."

"This from a profession that lives on fried ants and buttered scorpions?"

"Only in the field." Jackson was oblivious to the jape. He'd heard it too many times before.

"It may be the source of the hallucinations," Carter pointed out.

"We were experiencing altered realities before we consumed any native foods," Teal'C said. "That would seem to indicate that the food is harmless. Besides, the natives eat it without apparent harm."

"The natives don't exactly share our biology," O'Neill growled. But the argument made sense. The trees had walked long before they'd met any of the Kayeechi. He turned his attention to the Kayeechi with the energy staff.

"Eleb? Eleb, where did you get this?"

The brown-haired alien laughed as if at a tremendous joke. "We found it," he said. "Come and eat. Rejoice with us."

O'Neill took a deep breath. "If we eat with you, will you show us where you found these things?"

Vair laughed again. "Oh yes. And taste of this. It is very wonderful." He held out a flask.

O'Neill took it against his better judgment. Only the fact that none of the aliens had ventured anything like a threat against any of them—and a growing thirst—persuaded him to give the liquid a *very* tentative sip.

It *was* "very wonderful." It tasted of chocolate

and oranges, or cherries, and it had just enough of a bite to make it interesting. The bread was warm and flavored with honey and herbs, and the fruit was almost like Earth's, but just different enough to be intriguing. He sampled food and drink again, trying to identify the flavors, and a part of him noticed that he was relaxing. His better judgment didn't seem to matter quite so much any more.

The Kayeechi, once they realized just how interested the Earth team was in their possible weapons cache, were more than happy to drop hints and then change the subject, drawing them deeper and deeper into conversations about manners and tactics and life on P4V-837. The team ate and drank within the perfumed circle of friendly aliens, tried to encourage them to talk, passed their new flavor discoveries around. Shortly thereafter, they were all peacefully asleep once again, and the aliens crept quietly away.

Once more the water was cool against his skin, sliding soft and refreshing with the little movements he made to maintain his depth and equilibrium deep in the ocean. The cool flow was interrupted this time by an awkward belt arrangement; across his back he carried an energy staff, and at his side a zat gun.

The underwater coral city—it was more distinctly a city this time, with streets crammed with traffic, buildings with doors and windows—was still under seige. The invading octopi were still tearing at the buildings. The windows and doors were actually giving them a better grip. And beside him, Vair waved at his weapons, the alien's red hair floating through the water like a scarlet veil.

Clearly, he was supposed to help defend the city, using the weapons.

It wasn't his fight. He didn't know anything about this battle, and he had no intention of taking sides without more information.

In a hazy way, he knew he was dreaming, but he felt no particular desire to awaken.

Desperately, Vair reached for the energy staff, trying to tug it loose from the straps that held it in place across O'Neill's back. O'Neill pushed the alien away, and in their struggle, the staff came free and drifted down to the sandy seafloor. Vair dived after it, and O'Neill kicked hard to get there first. As he claimed the weapon, Vair took his hand and pointed.

Not ten meters away, one of the octopi had a small coral-creature in his tentacles, and the massive beak was poised to crunch through its skull.

O'Neill had a solid conviction that anybody

who was trying to kill a kid was by definition not a good guy. He raised the energy staff and fired.

The bolt of energy flashed, sizzled, and dissipated in the water.

He tried again.

For some reason, the staff wouldn't work. It felt heavy and clumsy. He reached for the zat gun and got the same result. The weapons were useless here, whether it was the water, the weapons themselves, or some other reason. He shook his head at Vair, dropped the gun, and dived toward the octopus, which was still floating serenely in the water, beak open, as if waiting for a cue to crunch. Vair squawked in protest or in disappointment—an interesting phenomenon underwater. He could feel rage from the alien, an almost overwhelming fury and urge to obliterate utterly the octopus and all its kind.

The next moment man and alien were standing in the middle of a desert, as dry as if they'd never been near a body of water in their lives, much less swimming through a battle in a coral sea.

It was oddly familiar too—nothing like the odd vegetation of P4V-837. He turned in place slowly, scanning the expanse of pale sand interrupted by patches of spiky grass and the occasional clump of prickly pear. That spray of fernlike stalks topped with tiny yellow flowers was flixweed. And that flicker of movement was a blue-tailed lizard taking shelter under a clump of Russian thistle.

The horizon was lumpy and uneven, as if someone had heaped up piles of mud in the distant past and then allowed them to slump down, almost but not quite returning to their original smooth surface. A ridge of hills made of sterner stuff jutted out baldly to the west, and he could just see a perfectly circular depression in the ground, perhaps a thousand yards wide, not far from its base.

It was the depression that tipped him off—that and the lizard of course. He'd seen shallow depressions or others like it before, flying Red Flag and Green Flag exercises on the Nellis Bombing and Gunnery Range in Nevada, where all the hotshot Air Force pilots played war simulations and dared each other to do—a small, reminiscent smile crossed his face—really, really stupid stunts. Flying over the Nevada Test Site, he'd seen quite a few of those perfectly circular pits in the earth. They looked as if some mad giant had punched upward from underneath the ground and then pulled back really fast, letting the earth collapse on itself.

Which in a sense was exactly what had happened.

He blinked, and then he was standing at the

bottom of a skeletal tower a hundred feet high. Next to him, a crane was lifting a large metal object upward. A crew of men stood nearby, watching anxiously. They didn't appear to see either O'Neill or his companion. Vair seemed to think the crane was fascinating, but his interest shifted to O'Neill when he realized the colonel couldn't care less about the moving machinery.

O'Neill recognized the object and the tower, and he knew where he was and that he was dreaming. He had to be. Nobody would let unauthorized personnel just stand around watching this.

Besides, this was— They didn't do this anymore. They hadn't done this for decades. This was like watching ancient history or a story from someone's memories of long ago.

The object was at least eight feet long, shaped like an extremely fat gray cigar. He could see the seams where the two ends had been welded together. He could hear the clanking of the heavy chains that raised it to the cradle, even though he couldn't quite distinguish the words that the observers yelled to the crane operator. The half dozen men at the foot of the tower, giving the crane operator his directions, were all wearing hard hats and sunglasses, white cotton shirts open at the throat, sleeves rolled up to the elbows. One man was still wearing a tie, though the knot had been loosened to halfway down his chest. He could see the drops of sweat on their foreheads beneath the rims of the hard hats, the shine of it on their chins. Not all the sweat was from the heat, he thought. It was early yet for it to be that hot.

The steel cigar swung alarmingly as the crane shifted position, and a thin whistle of apprehension came from one of the observers. Another laughed without humor and made some remark. No one responded.

The crew around the tower didn't notice O'Neill or his alien companion watching them from only a few feet away.

Or rather, O'Neill watched them; Vair, on the other hand, was watching O'Neill with a curious intensity.

There were wires coming off one end of the metal cigar, running down to the ground and off into the distance. The thing was inert so long as the wires weren't hot: just a lump of elements processed and polished and put together by the busy minds of men.

The cigar settled into a cradle at the top of the tower, and suddenly the crane and its operator were gone, the observers had vanished, and he could feel a cold chill running down his spine. They were standing at the foot of the tower, within touching distance of one of the metal supporting struts. He could see the rime of white, salty sand where someone had rested a sweating hand. The shadow of the massive metal shape above them fell across them, cooling them as only shadow in desert sunlight could do. They were alone with the tower, and he knew what that meant.

He desperately did not want to be here, not even in a dream. Vair was still watching him, occasionally looking up at the metal bulb above them. O'Neill turned away, wanting to run, knowing that it would do absolutely no good, and finally he could hear words clearly: *Five. Four. Three. Two. One*—

He was in the site observation and control room with the test crew. Why were there windows? There shouldn't be windows—

First the light, brighter than any words could describe, bright enough to let the blind see. Then the sound, an endless roar, and the impact of air displaced by a power too abrupt to comprehend.

The control room shattered, and so did he.

Ahhh, the watchers sighed.

Wooden claws made a peculiar sound, clacking against raw stone. Daniel Jackson looked up to see Anubis pawing at a painted image. A door swung open, and the wooden dog turned, panting happily, to look at him.

He was meant to follow. Of course.

Around him the sound of chanting and the scent of myrrh—no, that wasn't myrrh, it was some other incense—permeated the air, surging softly against his face as if moved by giant ostrich-feather fans. Before him Anubis trotted on, looking back expectantly every so often to make sure that Daniel was still with him.

Abruptly he found himself standing on one end of a narrow bridge. He reached for side rails and found nothing. He looked down and saw a dark stream, and sitting within it, directly under the bridge, a creature with the long jaws and jagged teeth of a crocodile, the body of a lion, and the hindquarters of a hippopotamus. *Am-Mit, the Devourer of Souls*. It was waiting for him to slip and fall.

Really, it made the Three Billy Goats Gruff look sad.

The creature looked up at him, grinned, and licked its lips. He swallowed hard. The creature continued to stare at him, its jaws parted in a grin, a line of saliva dripping from the corner of its mouth. Its eyes were round and yellow and had no depth at all.

He pulled himself away from its gaze with a jerk and tried to turn around, get back to safe ground. But there wasn't any safe ground any more; there wasn't anything behind him but shadows moving in darkness. The ground was gone.

In front of him stretched the narrow bridge, and on the other side, waiting even as the creature below waited, was a figure that looked like a man, but had the long, sharp curved beak of an ibis. He held scrolls of papyrus and an ancient pen in his hands, and stood next to a giant balance, two suspended bowls hanging from a T-bar.

In one of the bowls rested, ever so delicately, a large white feather. Its weight did not disturb the evenness of the balance in the least.

The wooden dog rose up on its hind legs and took on the body of a man, while retaining the shiny lacquered head of a jackal. "I bring you the Osiris Daniel," Anubis said to the ibis-headed man. "His heart is righteous, and it shall be weighed and shall not be found wanting. He has not sinned against any god or any goddess. I charge you to weigh him truly and all his deeds."

"*Ma'at*," Daniel whispered. The feather of truth against which the heart of a man was weighed to determine whether he would be thrown to the eager drooling jaws of Am-Mit or be permitted to live forever—he was in the middle of the Book of the Dead. The upright Anubis, then, was Upuaut, the Opener of the Ways. He would watch the scales to make sure that the heart was weighed fairly.

Movement behind the ibis-headed man—who could only be Thoth, the god of wisdom, lord of the Balance—attracted his attention. According to the text, this should be Osiris himself, lord of the dead, protector and judge, who lent his name to the dead who were brought before him. Osiris was one of the greatest of the Egyptian gods, perhaps the greatest of all. Jackson peered eagerly into the mists beyond the scales.

It was not Osiris, but Apophis who stood there—Apophis and Ra and all the other Goa'uld who had stolen Egyptian mythology. They were standing ankle deep in a shallow, wide pool of squirming dead-white Goa'uld larvae, waiting for him.

Thoth unrolled one of the scrolls, and from the ibis head came a human voice.

"Recite the laws of the gods and goddesses, and what you have done in your life that makes you worthy."

Revolted, he tried to step back, but Thoth was there, waiting.

Unbidden, words rose to his lips, words he had read the first time in translation as a child at his father's knee and at least once a year thereafter. They exerted a fascination that was, quite literally, timeless: thousands of years old and as true now as they ever had been:

> *What manner of land is this to which I have come? It has not water, nor air; it is depth unfathomable. It is black as the blackest night, and men wander lost and helpless. In it a man cannot live in quietness of heart; nor may the longings of love be satisfied. But let the state of the eternal be given unto me instead of water and air and the satisfying of the longings of love, and let quietness of heart be given unto me instead of cakes and ale.*

Sha're, he thought, despairing. The longings for that love would never be satisfied. The Book of the Dead described the bewilderment of the ka-soul in that empty place between life and life again while it waited to be judged by Thoth, the heart weighed against the feather of Truth.

He could not remember all the names of all the gods, the litany of all the sins he was supposed not to have committed during his life. There was something about not stealing bread either from children or from the gods, not stirring up strife or conspiring against the pharoah, not cursing or lying. He wasn't in the habit of terrorizing the innocent, but if Apophis was the pharoah, then he was doomed for all eternity.

Seeing his hesitation, Thoth reached out and

into him, sinking his immortal hand into Daniel's very flesh to open his side and remove his still beating heart to weigh it against the white feather.

And behind him, Apophis waited, smiling, and the larvae writhed and surged around him.

CHAPTER TEN

Daniel woke abruptly, shaking, moving from supine to upright in a single lunge. He felt frantically at his side. There was, of course, no wound, no gaping hole from which his heart had been extracted. The harsh sound of his panting slowed, and he swallowed, trying to work some moisture back into his mouth. Apophis was *dead*. How many times did he have to convince himself of that?

The rest of the team was sprawled asleep around him in the midst of debris from the meal the aliens had brought. The Kayeechi themselves had vanished, taking with them their weapons, but he could see Teal'C's staff lying at his side, and the sidearms and rifles were still exactly where they belonged. Everything was quiet; he could hear insects and the sound of the breeze in the trees, the heavy breathing of his teammates, but nothing else. Still shaken by the vivid dream, he took a couple of deep breaths and nearly choked on the scent of smouldering incense. In search of some fresh air, he stepped carefully around the others and stepped outside the circle of ceremonial incense toward the mouth of the cave.

His path took him straight through the middle of the little glen where they had eaten with the Kayeechi—or it should have. As soon as he left the cave, he found himself walking on a beach, the white sand crunching under his feet, seagulls squabbling in the air overhead, the smell of salt strong in his nostrils. The sun was hot on his fair skin. He stopped dead. " 'And that was odd,' " he quoted softly to himself, " 'for it was the middle of the night.' "

This place did seem rather like something out of Alice in Wonderland. He looked behind him, but the cave and his sleeping companions were gone.

"I must still be asleep," he said and then wondered how he could be asleep and talking to himself about it. He shrugged. Dreams weren't supposed to be rational. This one seemed even "realer," if possible, than the last one, walking through a tomb, reading the wall paintings, actually experiencing— He shook his head abruptly. This world was just *odd*. He was beginning to think that O'Neill's usual paranoia about such things really was appropriate here, although that raised another interesting question. Why *were* they still here? As soon as the team realized that they weren't all seeing the same things, O'Neill should have pulled them out. If you couldn't trust your own eyes—or the eyes of the person guarding your back—you shouldn't be hanging around. Period. Even with the lure of a warehouse full of Goa'uld weapons somewhere nearby, it wasn't worth it.

Yet here they were, still, eating and drinking like starving Persephones. And sleeping. He supposed Persephone slept during her visits to Hades. He wondered if she dreamed.

He stepped out, enjoying the feel of the sand and the sun. If nothing else, this particular delusion was providing some decent exercise. He wondered how far he was from the cave. He wondered if he had ever left it at all.

Whether he had or not, at the moment he was standing on a beach, with an ocean on his left and a tropical forest on his right, and a bright white stretch of beach in front of him. As he watched a wave recede, he could see some tiny form of sea life burrowing madly into the sand, making a V shape in the retreating water.

He was definitely going to tell Jack they ought to leave this nuthouse of a world as fast as possible. It was fascinating, sure, and he had never had such vivid dreams, but there was just something *wrong* here.

The sound of the sea to his left got louder, as if the waves were becoming more insistent. Pausing, he shaded his eyes with one hand to see better. There was definitely something going on up there. It was a woman, and she was naked. Was it Sha're?

For a moment hope and vision blurred, and he saw the olive skin and lustrous black hair of his late wife, the passion of his life. She was standing only a hundred meters away, facing him, her arms lifted, waiting for him.

He began to run.

The image blurred sharply, as if someone had changed a channel, and he stopped running. Everything was the same except—

It was *Carter*.

And she wasn't waiting for him with open arms. She was turned away, facing out to sea, and on one knee in a shooting position. She had a zat gun in her hand and was sighting along the barrel at something in the water, firing repeatedly, retreating in a backward scrabble and raising her angle of fire as she did so.

He didn't stop to wonder what Carter was doing on the beach nude. She was fighting something rising up out of the water, and whatever it was seemed about to overwhelm her. He shook himself. This *had* to be a dream.

And if it was a dream, dammit, he liked the last version better. He blinked, trying to bring back the image of his wife.

Once again the image blurred and shuddered, and for an instant, was Sha're again, this time wearing a Hawaiian lei and sarong, crowned with flowers as she had been on the day he had married her, according to the customs of her people, although the lei and sarong hadn't featured then. She'd worn the dress of her people, descended from Middle Eastern desert nomads— and the image blurred once more, and it was Carter again.

And he could see the mountain of kraken looming over her.

He bit the inside of his lower lip and tasted blood. And it *hurt*. He spat out a mouthful of reddened saliva and began running down the beach to help his teammate.

As close as he came, Carter didn't seem to hear him calling, even when he arrived at her side. He could see red marks appearing on her skin where the Thing struck at her and connected, sending her sprawling across the sand. She reached up, her face twisted with rage and determination, and held out her hand, palm out; a ribbon of power lanced out at the crea-

ture, and it changed, solidified, grew into a
mountain soaring impossibly high over their
heads. As he watched, Carter was suddenly
dressed in alpine gear, the ribbon weapon still
wrapped around her heavy ski glove. He gazed
up the slope to the lip of snow at the top of the
mountain as its crest trembled, quivered, and
shelved off in a massive avalanche thundering
down at them.

*What is that? The human did not choose that
weapon the last time.*

*I can't see what it is. It looks like something
wrapped around her hand.*

Look closer. Make him look closer!

He stepped back, away from the lash of the
Goa'uld ribbon weapon and away from the
avalanche—Carter was running away, still with
no sign she knew he was there—when he found
himself struggling for air, submerged in an un-
dersea city with no idea how he'd gotten there
or where the surface was. Instead of running
along sand he was kicking frantically at water.
There was no mountain, no avalanche, no
Carter. He gasped and took in a lungful of fluid.
Around him, he was dimly aware of movement,
but the most important thing, the only thing at
the moment, was getting air. His chest felt as if
someone had fastened a vise around him and
was squeezing it tighter and tighter, about to

crush him from sheer pressure. He kept kicking, desperate to find the surface. He was getting dizzy from lack of air, beginning to hear voices in the thudding of the bubbles of air escaping from his lungs.

What is he doing? He isn't supposed to waken!

He is in the midst of the Shaping, and I cannot control where he goes. I don't understand—

Etra'ain, if you cannot control him, let him walk. There was a weapon there we could have used to crush the Narrai and burn their nestlings. Are you growing weak? Do we need another Shaper?

The response was immediate and sharp as Etra'ain pulled her attention away from what he was doing to face her challenger. *Do you propose to replace me? Can you do what I do?*

And then he really was pulling air and not liquid into his lungs, and his arms and legs were beating a frantic tattoo against the dry earth of the cave where they'd made camp. He stilled himself and lay stunned, trying to understand what was happening to him, not moving except for the heaving of his chest as he pulled oxygen past the raw tissues of his nose and throat. His tongue probed gingerly at the raw place where he'd bitten his lip to try to wake himself up. It was still bleeding.

Perhaps we should! Are you doing anything at all?

I provided Shapes we could touch and feel.

Those are little things. Small things. You are very good at little things, Etra'ain.

You know what I can do, Shasee. And if you have forgotten, observe!

Having tentatively decided that as long as he didn't go anywhere he was probably not going anywhere, Daniel pulled himself into a tight ball, wrapped his arms around his knees, and looked at his peacefully sleeping teammates. The position reminded him unpleasantly of the vise imagery, and he bounced to his feet instead, teetering dangerously in his effort not to step in any direction. He didn't want to know where he'd find himself next.

Perhaps they weren't sleeping so peacefully after all, he thought after a moment. There was Carter—fully dressed in regular camouflage fatigues, and he could feel himself blushing hotly—lying asprawl a backpack, her face twitching and her hands clenching and unclenching as if she were wrapping and unwrapping something around them.

Teal'C was frowning even more deeply than usual, if that were possible. He was sleeping at attention practically, with his arms straight at his sides. It looked supremely uncomfortable.

And O'Neill—if the man had been upright he'd be setting records for the hundred yard dash. He was gasping as if he were running too, and his face twisted with an expression difficult to read.

Jackson pushed a lock of hair out of his face and thought long and hard.

He was reasonably sure that he was, at this moment at least, awake. But then he thought he'd been awake when he was drowning too, and his clothing was completely dry. His lip was still bleeding though. He couldn't tell any more. If he was awake, why was he the only one? Was he awake? Or was this another dream?

It was too weird, he decided. They had to get out of this place, fast, whether they were dreaming or waking. Hidden supply of offworld weapons be damned. How would they even know what they had when they found it, if they ever did? He reached over and picked up a clod of dirt from the mouth of the cave, crumbling the encrusted dirt off one edge and sifting it between his fingers, rubbing the silicate grains into his fingertips. It was real—felt real, smelled real even—he touched it gingerly to his tongue and made a face—tasted real. He drew a deep breath and tossed it the few feet across the little picnic ground at O'Neill.

The clod shattered an inch in front of the other man's face, and Jackson winced.

Rather than waking up, O'Neill twitched his

nose and upper lip and batted one hand at his face, as if to dislodge a particularly annoying insect. Then, groaning, he rolled over so that his back was to the rest of the team.

Jackson shook his head. All right. Raw sandy fingers and the taste of dirt said he was awake, but an O'Neill who slept that heavily was against nature. He'd been standing watches with the colonel for years now, and if there was one thing certain in the universe, it was that Jack O'Neill was a light sleeper. If he were drugged, he wouldn't have reacted to the dirt clod. So this *must* be a dream.

He was fairly certain that there was a hole in his logic somewhere, but by this time he had too much adrenaline in his system to try to get back to sleep or to dreaming, whichever was appropriate. It looked as if, in this part of his consciousness, he was elected to stand watch, since no one else was volunteering—another indication that he was dreaming, no doubt.

O'Neill had fallen asleep on watch. Jackson wondered if the colonel had thought he was awake all the while.

Cautiously, he took one tentative step toward the cave, then another, pausing to look up at the brilliant blue sky. The moons hung in the east, pale in this season against the glare of this world's sun. It certainly looked like daytime.

"All right," he said to himself. Looking around, he eyed a convenient outcropping of rock, took up position, and kicked at it as hard as he could.

He had to stuff his hand in his mouth to keep from cursing at the pain. If he hadn't been wearing combat boots, he would have broken his foot. Tears started up in his eyes as he caught himself on the rim of rock at the mouth of the cave and gingerly wiggled the abused toes. He was not dreaming, dammit.

The rest of the team slept on in the little clearing.

Setting the foot carefully on the ground, he limped forward a couple of yards, so focused on testing the foot's ability to bear weight that he didn't immediately notice the change in the surface it rested upon.

He was standing on a slope.

On a ramp. A steel ramp. A very familiar steel ramp.

In the middle of the Gate room.

But the Gate room had never stunk like this before.

At least, not in his own universe. There'd been another Gate room once, in an alternate Earth, where O'Neill had commanded—

Take three deep breaths and you won't notice the stink anymore, one of his professors had told him in graduate school. The advice had been meant for a young man who'd grown up in the relatively sterile world of Western culture, whose first encounter with the realities of new cultures could be overwhelming. He hadn't needed it, growing up with parents who spent their professional lives on digs. Those parents had died early in his life, but he remembered what it was like to live in places on other continents and in other cultures.

He'd always thought that particular professor was full of it. The advice had never worked, and even now, when he tried it yet again out of habit, he only managed to inhale the scent of smoke and burning plastic, discharged weapons and death.

Bodies were sprawled before him, all wearing uniforms and bearing the signs of intense energy beams targeted on human flesh.

He limped down the ramp and listened, holding his breath now as much to shut out the smell as the distraction.

He could hear machinery humming, the faint crackle of exposed and shorting-out wiring. Turning, he could see the depthless surface of the Stargate shimmering, waiting.

He was morally certain he had not come here through a wormhole. For one thing, he wasn't cold, and he was *always* cold from travel through the Gate.

And besides, the Gate on P4V-837 was far from the cave and its apron of grass where they had eaten their breakfast/lunch with the Kay-eechi.

Gate or not, he was home. In a manner of speaking. Cheyenne Mountain was as close to "home" as he got.

Something horrible had happened here.

He rested his hand on his sidearm and moved farther into the room, stepping around the bodies and the ruined machinery, avoiding the sightless stares of the dead, but recognizing them nonetheless.

That was Jolley, one of the technicians, and that squad over there, he'd played cards with them one night—they were good losers.

Their blood was dried and black on the metal floor. The bodies had been lying here for some time—long enough for putrification to set in, long enough for bloating, long enough to smell.

He swallowed and stepped to the door, afraid for a moment that the electronic locks had shorted out and he would find himself shut in with the Gate and the dead; but to his relief the door opened smoothly, and he found himself in a corridor scarred with deep black slashes in walls and ceiling and floor.

There was still no human sound, only the humming of fluorescent lights. His own foot-steps were louder, came faster as he began to trot down the hallway, ignoring the pain in his foot.

In the briefing room, he found Hammond slumped in his chair. He had been unarmed. So had most of the staff in the room. What few weapons there were hadn't been nearly enough.

It was Goa'uld—it had to be. He had seen what happened to worlds where the Goa'uld had unleashed their Jaffa minions to know the signs. The burns were from the slash of energy staffs. The other damage was, if not from the same staffs, from similar weapons the Jaffa wielded.

He left the briefing room and headed for the infirmary, certain that if there were any sur-vivors they would be there—but once again he found only the dead. Janet Frasier lay behind an overturned lab table, a gun still clutched in her hand. Not far away he found the bodies of three of her staff and a couple of patients—and that of Amanda Carter.

It stopped him cold. He fell to his knees beside her, lifting her lax form, brushing the blond hair out of her eyes. It was impossible. Carter was on

P4V-837, with the rest of the team, not here. And he was here, not there . . . . Choking, he pressed her eyelids shut and laid her back down again, straightening her limbs carefully, tugging the remains of the battle jacket over the bloody mess that had been her abdomen.

"I want to wake up," he whispered, getting to his feet. "I'm dreaming. I know I'm dreaming, and *I want to wake up!*"

There was no response, no change in his surroundings. The complex was silent save for the murmur of abandoned machinery. The smell of decay was almost visible, far stronger, in fact, than the apparent decomposition of the bodies would warrant.

He spun and ran out of the infirmary. The elevators were still working; he took them to the living area, where a number of the Stargate team members maintained residence in between missions. The doors to the individual rooms stood open; again, blackened swaths and smears of blood testified to a slaughter. The only bodies he found were human ones; whatever had done this had taken their casualties away with them. The Complex had never seemed so large to him before, and he had never felt so alone in it.

He found O'Neill's body in the officer's mess, his rifle still in his hands, along with a half dozen others. Several of the other bodies were burned and torn. As far as he could see, there had been two groups of humans here: one being ripped apart and the other merely destroyed. O'Neill had belonged to the latter group, apparently leading a rescue mission that had failed. The rifle told him that the colonel had had enough warning to get to the arms lockers. It hadn't been such a short battle after all.

He stepped across the bodies to the bar, and in the process, a glint of light caught his eye—a reflection off a shard of glass. He bent over and saw a mat of light hair, one pale lock sticking out of a thick, dark, gummy mat. The mat was attached to a body.

He looked closer and saw himself, half under a table, facedown, head pulped and misshapen from a heavy blow. He'd been a member of the first group, the ones O'Neill had tried to rescue, and there were no weapons in his hands. His feet were tied together. His clothing was soaked in stiff, dried black blood.

Under the circumstances, he felt that vomiting was an entirely reasonable response. He just managed to avoid doing so all over his own corpse. At least "his" eyes were closed. He wasn't sure if he could have handled staring into his own— No, he wasn't even going to think about it. He wasn't going to let this nightmare get the better of him.

At least his face—his dead face—was serene, even if it was only the serenity that came from muscles relaxed by—

Grabbing a bottle of alcohol from the cabinet behind the bar was entirely reasonable too. At least one glass-fronted window had survived the carnage, and he reached in while steadfastly ignoring the mirror behind it.

The sharp taste of good whiskey shocked him; after one long swallow, the bottle fell from his trembling hands, shattering on the floor, splashing over his fatigues and boots. He jumped at the sound.

"Alternate universe," he said, ignoring the fact that there was no one left to hear but himself. "Okay. It's an alternate. That's what it is. I'm dreaming of an alternate universe, and that's an alternate me and an alternate Jack and Janet and Sam and—it's not us—

"But how the hell did I get here and *how can I get back*?"

The sound of rising hysteria did as much as the drink had to help bring himself back under control. He'd been in alternate universes before—maybe, he realized, even this very one. This could very well be the universe where the Goa'uld had invaded. He hadn't seen any sign of

Teal'C among the bodies, and he was morally certain that the Jaffa he knew wouldn't have allowed the others to die without him.

It was somehow steadying to think of it that way, but that still left the problem of why he'd found himself here. In that other universe, he'd never been a part of the Stargate project.

It didn't really matter. So what if this was still another variation in an endless procession of not quite identical Earths? In one the Jaffa had invaded at the behest of the Goa'uld. In another, Teal'C had killed his own alternate version. In this one, all the human members of the team, himself included, had died. He supposed he could go back and check rank, see if Hammond still outranked O'Neill or vice versa, but what difference would it make? They were still dead. He, on the other hand, was still alive, at least for the time being. He took a long, steadying breath and stepped around the bodies. He'd arrived in this universe in the Gate room. Maybe the way back was by the same path.

He was passing a cross corridor, retracing his steps, when he thought he heard voices, and before he had a chance to reason it out, he flattened himself against the wall. The voices went on, neither rising nor falling in volume, and he relaxed slightly and began edging toward them.

They were coming from one of the ready

rooms. He was within a few yards when he realized that he was hearing the sound of a television set, a news announcer making a report. He stopped just outside the door, ready to bolt if he caught sight of almost anything alive.

As far as he could tell, the room was empty. He could see a corner of the television image, and he edged nearer, improving his line of sight.

"Washington, D.C. is recovering from the initial devastation of the long anticipated reprisal, if recovering *is a word that can be used in this context."* The voice was British; the BBC-1 logo appeared in the lower right-hand corner of the screen, and the images shown by the panning camera revealed the Capitol in smoking blackened ruins beneath a lowering sky. At least there were signs of life in the streets: a dark sedan maneuvered its way between wrecked vehicles, the Washington Monument pristine and untouched in the background; a party of rescuers carried stretchers down the steps of the Supreme Court building. The cameras focused on the face of a weeping mother, a shocked and silent policeman, and then moved on, pausing at the gap in the dome of the Capitol Building, letting Jackson get a good look at the semicircular hole. It was as if a giant genie had taken a bite out of an apple or shot a zat gun at a giant kraken.

"There is of course no way of knowing if this is the last lesson the Goa'uld will see fit to administer to a rebellious United States. World leaders agreed that the loss of Philadelphia and San Francisco should have been enough to convince the American President of the overwhelming technical superiority of the Goa'uld, but her advisors evidently disagreed, with predictable consequences . . . ."

A burst of static interrupted the transmission, and he stepped closer.

"On the home front, His Majesty's Government have made all efforts to ensure that no such dreadful fate shall befall—"

Jackson moved inside the ready room, looking for the remote to turn the damned thing off. But he promptly tripped over the recumbent body of a snoring Jack O'Neill, who was lying exactly where he'd been left, in a cave on a world called P4V-837.

I can walk through dreams. I can take the waking ones through the Shaping of those dreams. I blend the dreams. You see what I have done. Can you do as much, Vair? Do you challenge me still?

Elsewhere on that world, a red-furred alien raised one hand in a gesture of temporary defeat, acknowledging the mastery of the one sitting opposite him in the Circle of Shaping.

With a regal nod, Etra'ain released the Shape

of the world so that her Circle could return to the village.

Once they were gone and she was alone in her own place, surrounded by her own things made with her own hands—not a single Shape among them—she sagged, once more exhausted and sickened by what she had created from what she had seen in the minds and the dreams of the Tall Ones.

CHAPTER ELEVEN

This time, at least, O'Neill reacted as expected. The colonel woke abruptly and completely, grabbing Jackson by the ankle and pulling him down, twisting to bring himself up to deliver an elbow strike to the throat.

"Awk!" Jackson could only raise his hands in a futile effort to ward off the blow, but by that time, O'Neill had recognized him and let him go, falling back to a sitting position and holding his head in his hands.

Daniel lay quivering. He was going to have a breakdown after this mission, he promised himself. He'd worked hard for it, he'd earned it, and nobody was going to take it away from him. And he was damned if he was going to be killed twice on the same day.

"Uh, sorry about that," O'Neill said, looking up at last.

"Hey, no problem." The archaeologist sat up

and brushed himself off. He could still smell the odor of decay and Scotch whiskey on his clothing, and he gagged.

"Are you okay?" O'Neill asked at once.

Jackson raised a hand to reassure him and fend off any misplaced sympathies. As he did so, O'Neill took a puzzled sniff. "That's whiskey," he said. "Where'd you get it?" And then, startled, he looked around and up at the position of the sun in the sky. "Don't tell me we fell asleep again!"

"I think we'd better talk," Jackson said, finally recovering a measure of his mental equilibrium. "All of us. Now."

Since Jackson made no move to implement his own suggestion, O'Neill aroused the others. Carter and Teal'C were equally startled and dismayed to discover they had been sleeping in the middle of the day—indeed, in the middle of the picnic—and once again they took a thorough inventory of their weapons and supplies, only to find, once again, nothing missing at all.

When they were all gathered in a circle in the sunlight at the cave entrance, O'Neill raised an expectant eyebrow. "Okay, you've got the floor, Daniel. Do you have some idea what's going on? Other than this being the most *restful* damn mission we've ever been on."

"It's the dreams," he began, then stopped, trying to figure out how to go on. His audience leaned forward intently.

"I thought I was awake, but maybe I wasn't," he said. There was still a raw place on his inner lip though, and it still hurt. He exhaled sharply. "I'm not sure it matters.

"I had a dream. Woke me up. At least I thought it woke me up. So I got up—I have no idea how long ago—and thought I'd go get some fresh air." He waved one hand vaguely at the remains of the food, still piled on the picnic mat. It was now attracting the local flies. "At least I thought I was going for a little walk." He swallowed hard and stretched his neck, staring at the empty ceiling overhead, not wanting to meet his teammates' eyes. "I stepped out of this clearing and I was on a beach. Gorgeous place, with white sand and palm trees and blue skies. It was daylight—high noon in fact." He glanced over at Carter, and then immediately away, hoping that the shadow cast by the hill hid the heat in his face. "I saw you there. You were fighting something, shooting at it with a zat gun. It looked like a giant squid, one of those things they say live at the bottom of the ocean that eat sperm whales for snacks. It was almost on the beach and hitting at you with its tentacles. You were firing back at it with a zat gun, at first, and then a Goa'uld ribbon weapon. And when you killed it, there was a tsunami. And the wave changed into a mountain."

"That was *my* dream!" Carter exclaimed. "I didn't see you there! That's exactly what happened. But I thought I was all alone on that island. What—"

Her words suddenly registered on her, and she fell silent, confused and a little embarrassed as more details came back to her.

"I tried to reach you, but when I came toward you all of a sudden I was underwater." O'Neill straightened up at this. "There was this city—coral, I think. I couldn't see much of it because, well, I was drowning." He gave them a twisted smile. "Never did like deep water. Anyway, I was trying to swim to the surface and all of a sudden I was lying in the middle—"

"Of a desert," O'Neill said grimly. "Am I right?" At the expressions of the others, he added, "That was *my* dream." The colonel turned back to Jackson. "Then what happened?"

"I woke up here," Jackson said simply. "At least, I think I did." He bit his lip and winced. "I figured I was just having funny dreams, maybe a reaction to the food or something. So I tried again going out for some fresh air, and—" He shuddered, forced himself to continue, looking directly at Teal'C. "I stepped out of here and I was in the Gate room back on Earth. Only it wasn't our Earth. There had been a huge battle, and everybody was dead. You were"—he nodded to Carter—"and Hammond and Frasier and you, Jack, and even me. I found me. But not you, Teal'C. I didn't find you anywhere."

His hands were still shaking, he noticed with detached interest.

"It was the Goa'uld," he said. "It was real. The look—the *smell* of it—it was all real. But it wasn't our Earth because we're here, not there, but we were there and we were dead."

"You didn't happen to pour yourself a stiff drink in that dream, did you?" O'Neill asked dryly. "Because you're a little more aromatic than you were this afternoon, I'm telling you."

Before Daniel could answer, Teal'C spoke up. "You were in my dream the last time, Daniel Jackson," the Jaffa said. "I dreamed I was in the service of Apophis, and we had invaded Earth. I killed you. I am pleased to find it was not so."

"Not as pleased as we are. Alternate universe maybe?" O'Neill wondered aloud.

"I thought of that, Jack, but how'd I get there? You were dreaming it. I was *there*."

"And they *were* dreams." The colonel shook his head. "They had to be. I remember that underwater stuff. I had Vair following me around like a tour director, but I didn't see you."

"But how? And why?" Daniel asked.

"It's those damned apples," O'Neill specu-lated. "It's always the apples in the Garden of Paradise. But that doesn't tell us why."

"It looks like somehow, outside of this cave, our dreams are real," Carter said slowly. "And you know what, it's not just us. I'll bet that's why we saw things right out of the Gate."

"Perhaps this is merely a characteristic of this world," Teal'C said. "I do not think it could be the food we ate. We saw strange things as soon as we set foot on this planet."

"Maybe so, but it doesn't make it a prime tourist spot in my opinion." O'Neill got to his feet. "We're heading for home, folks. Right now. I don't care what resources this world has or how many Goa'uld weapons might be hidden away. We are *outta* here." His whole attitude ex-uded relief that he finally was able to say it with-out any reservations whatsoever.

Daniel eyed the clearing outside the cave and shook his head. His face was still pale with shock. "I don't know, Jack. *Can* we get home?"

O'Neill winced. "Good point. But if we're all awake and all stick together, we ought to be able to get back to the Gate."

"If we really *are* all awake," Daniel muttered. "How can we tell?"

"All right, so maybe we can't. But if we aren't,

we're going to sign up for a joint hallucination. We *will* all see the same thing."

As one, the team decided not to examine that particular resolution too closely, and gathered up their packs and supplies.

They stuck close together as they ventured out of the cave, by common consent keeping Daniel in the middle of their little band. He was having trouble enough trusting reality without venturing more than a couple of feet away from the rest of them. But of all of them he was the least surprised when, once out of the clearing, they found the morning sun—which nanoseconds ago had been in late-afternoon phase—shining brightly down upon them.

"'And that was odd, the Walrus said,'" O'Neill began.

"'For it was the middle of the night,'" Carter took up the rest of the verse.

Daniel couldn't bring himself to comment. He was still shaking convulsively, jumping at every little noise, looking quickly from side to side as if to catch some fleeting glimpse of some other reality ducking behind every tree. Teal'C merely filed the exchange away as one more odd Earth thing to figure out someday.

Shasee! Shasee, Vair, Eleb, they are leaving the cave!

*The Shape has collapsed. Where is Etra'ain? Go
and get her. We must stop them.*

With effort, the teammates retraced their path
to the village where they had first feasted with
the Kayeechi. They were uneasily aware that
they were being watched—the sudden stillness
of birds and the residual trembling of a tree
branch were enough to tell them that, whether it
was seen as an oak tree or a fern or a lilac bush.
None of them reported seeing any cities, though
Daniel in particular kept searching for his crystal
tower.

They had crested the last rise, and the Gate itself was in sight, when the Kayeechi rose up out
of the grassy brush all around them. The team
formed a circle, back to back to back to back, to
meet them, weapons ready.

"Why are you here?" Shasee asked plaintively,
trotting up to O'Neill and stopping only when
the colonel raised his rifle across his chest in a
clearly defensive move. "You aren't supposed to
be here. You're supposed to be at the sleeping
place. Please, go back. Do you not wish to
see—"

"Thanks, but we've had just about enough of
your hospitality," O'Neill informed him. "We're
going home now. If we're ever back in the neigh-
borhood, we'll say hi."

"No. You *must* stay. You have much to teach

us." Even on the alien face, the expression of anxiety was easy to read. Shasee was frightened, and not of the weapons the visitors to his world were holding.

The Kayeechi kept crowding forward, a rainbow of small furry creatures.

"Keep moving to the Gate," O'Neill said out of the corner of his mouth, and the phalanx of SG-1 took a step closer to the DHD. The Kayeechi had surrounded them, six or seven deep, but gave way unconsciously to the physical pressure of the movement.

They were giving way to another pressure as well. O'Neill could see the aliens looking back over their shoulders at some of the newcomers and then parting to welcome them. He could track their progress by the movement of the natives, but meanwhile, he kept the team moving, one unobtrusive step at a time.

The newcomers had finally made it to the front of the crowd, facing them. One, with thin lines of purple fur crosshatched over her face, stepped clear of the rest, and Shasee and the others gave way in obvious deference. The murmurs of the crowd faded out as the aliens listened, and the progress toward the DHD halted.

"I am Etra'ain," Purplehatch announced, as if this in itself was supposed to awe them. It certainly awed the Kayeechi, or at least most of them. "I am she who Shapes. You cannot leave. We have need of you. You know this is true."

"Shapes? You're shaped like a Teletubby," O'Neill said pleasantly, if not correctly. "And no, I don't know it's true. I don't know what you're talking about. It's been fun, the meals were great, and now we're going home."

Etra'ain looked as distressed as Shasee had, her small hands twisting around each other. "But you *must* know. You have seen the battles. You have fought with us. We will be destroyed if you leave." She walked around their circle, looking each of them in the eye. "You," she said to Daniel. "You are a wise man who seeks justice. You walked in the Shapings. You," she addressed Teal'C, "are a man who knows what it is to lead armies and conquer.

"You," she said to Carter, "are a man who is resourceful and inventive. You all have much to offer, much more than you have given us already. We need you."

"I think you have a few of the details wrong," Carter muttered indignantly.

"Don't get me wrong, I think you're very nice people," O'Neill said with considerable patience, "but we can't stay here. We can't trust our senses, and that puts us in danger. You may not understand that, but it's very important to us that we see reality."

The aliens muttered to each other, and Vair and Shasee approached Etra'ain and spoke to her directly. When they had finished and stepped back out of her way, she sighed and nodded. "I understand. You wish to see the—" She tilted her head. "There is no word for it in your language."

"Try," O'Neill encouraged.

" 'Reality'?" she said tentatively. "We don't understand the term."

"We want to see things as they are," Daniel said. "Each one of us sees something—a tree, for instance—as a different thing. If we were looking at reality, each of us would be seeing the same thing."

Again, the aliens muttered to each other.

"To all see the same thing, you would all have to be the same person," Etra'ain protested. "How could this be? Each mind is different. Each spirit is different. How can the world be the same to all of you?"

The team looked over their shoulders at each other blankly. "Boy, wouldn't you like to meet this world's Einstein?" Carter asked. "Imagine what their Theory of Relativity must be like!"

"I think we *are* meeting this world's Einstein," Daniel said. "Look."

Vair and Shasee had returned, bearing small covered pots with slits in the lids. Smoke curled out. The two aliens were wearing masks to keep from inhaling it.

"If you wish to be all of one mind," Etra'ain said with distaste, "we can make it so for a little time. We can give you the clear sight with *mor'ee-rai*. But you must stay with us, for you are very strange and different and you can aid us. You can save us. We need you."

"Wait a minute. What's that stuff?" O'Neill demanded as Etra'ain gestured and Vair held the little container up to him and whipped off the top. As he did so, the entire mass of Kayeechi took a deep breath and blew, as if putting out a giant birthday cake. Their combined breath pushed the smoke of the burning incense into their faces. "Hey!"

Daniel sneezed, as did Teal'C. Carter made a face and waved a hand to get the smoke out of her eyes, but it was too late for all of them.

Like a shelf of snow falling off a mountain or a curtain being taken from a window, the valley around them changed. They were still surrounded by a crowd of Kayeechi, but everything else was different. Even the Kayeechi themselves were different. Several were heavily bandaged, and some required the support of others to walk. Most of them wore expressions that the team had seen all too often on too many worlds, including their own: shock, weariness, and pain.

The four members of SG-1 stepped apart, looking around.

"Teal'C, what do you see?" O'Neill asked.

"Signs of battle," the Jaffa responded promptly. "Much of the vegetation has been burned off, and there are bodies in the near distance piled as for a pyre . . . ."

"There's a trench dug in front of them," Carter added, turning around. "There are two distinct kinds of aliens represented: one like the Kay-eechi and another that looks like some kind of . . ."

"Octopus," Daniel took up the description. "A land octopus holding clubs in multiple arms."

"And the smell—my God," Carter said. "Burning. Decay . . ."

"You can taste it in the air," Jackson added. "But is it real? Or are we dreaming again? Hallucinating?"

"When one has many alternate possibilities to choose from, all equally valid, reality is what you choose to be real," Teal'C said. "This time, we share the reality. Therefore, it *is* real."

"An existentialist Jaffa," O'Neill muttered. "That's *all* I need."

"This is a battlefield," Teal'C said, ignoring

the colonel. "You said that you had disputes with your neighbors. This is the result."

"You see," Etra'ain said, covering the pot again. "You all see the same thing, although we sorrow to make this so. But you must understand that we are at war. Those we fight are evil and we must destroy them."

"We're not going to fight your war for you." O'Neill was quite definite about that.

"You need not," she responded. "You need only continue to share your knowing of your world. You have wonderful things."

"We're not going to tell you—and just telling wouldn't do any good anyway."

"Oh my God," Jackson said, interrupting. "That's it. The staff and the zat gun. They're getting the weapons out of our dreams. They're using our dreams to create reality."

"That's ridiculous," O'Neill said.

As he spoke, six of the aliens gathered behind Etra'ain produced zat guns and aimed them awkwardly at the team.

"Um, you don't suppose they got those at the local K-Mart?" Jackson asked.

One of the guns went off, startling all of them. Fortunately or otherwise, the beam struck one of the other aliens, who screamed and crumpled, thrashing on the ground. The other Kayeechi milled around frantically. More beams flashed.

The team began to return fire, aiming by common consent over the aliens' heads, as they retreated to the Gate. The diminutive folk produced energy staffs and began hauling them up to fire, even though it sometimes took two of them to hold one weapon. As Jackson activated the Gate, the alien aim improved. Bolts of energy from both staff and zat guns began to punch holes in the air uncomfortably close to their heads.

O'Neill crumpled. Teal'C promptly hauled him over a shoulder and they stepped through the wormhole.

CHAPTER TWELVE

The signal that opened the protective iris at Stargate Command on Earth also triggered a buzz of activity at the core of the complex. The twenty-four–hour guard stood poised in case a hostile party had gained access to the iris trigger. A medical team mobilized to administer immediate aid to potential incoming casualties. Notification was sent immediately to General George Hammond that someone, presumably and hopefully one of the Stargate teams, was arriving.

All of this was standard operating procedure. Thus, when SG-1 stumbled through the Gate, with Teal'C carrying the stunned O'Neill like a rag doll, a shock cart was standing by, and before Carter had managed to get to the end of the ramp, the colonel was on his way to the infirmary. An officious lieutenant counted the remaining three noses on the team and demanded, "Any other injuries?"

Teal'C, Jackson, and Carter looked at each other and at the reassuringly familiar surroundings of the Gate room and shook their heads.

"It was a zat gun," Jackson called after the departing gurney. One of the enlisted personnel moving the recumbent officer along raised a hand in acknowledgment.

"Threat condition?" asked the captain of the watch, shooing the medical lieutenant out of the way.

The team members looked at each other again. "Uh, not high," Jackson ventured.

"There is no immediate danger to Earth or the Gate," Teal'C clarified. "I do not believe the natives are capable of understanding Gate technology or are in a position to launch an attack."

"Agreed," Carter said. "How's the colonel?"

The iris had snapped shut, and the Gate guard detachment stood down. The murmur of voices in the background indicated that the preliminary report was being passed along to Stargate Command.

"Wouldn't know. You'd better go ask," the captain said.

Carter looked up at the observation deck. "I think we'd like to find out. And maybe get cleaned up before we debrief," she said.

General Hammond, who was watching from the glassed-in vantage point above, saw the question in her expression and the utter weariness in the three team members. As he stood there, an aide passed along the immediate rundown from Medical. He sighed and nodded to the team below, then waited to get the whole story.

In the infirmary, Janet Frasier reviewed Jack O'Neill's vital signs, observed the twitching of his eyelids, and compared the symptoms to previous examples of similar injuries she'd treated in the years that the Stargate had been in operation. After giving all of this her due and professional consideration, she pulled up a chair beside the bed and took O'Neill's hand in hers and waited for her patient to wake up.

It took long enough for her to begin to wonder about her chosen treatment protocol, but eventually the man in the bed stirred and muttered a curse. Smiling, the doctor glanced down the empty row of beds in the small ward. Sometimes the whole room was full of curses or, worse, moans and cries of wounded soldiers. This was highly preferable, all things considered.

O'Neill stirred and cursed again, more loudly.

Satisfied that his recovery was proceeding as expected, Janet relinquished his hand and began taking vitals all over again. By the time she finished, his brown eyes were open and watching her.

"I suppose I'm hooked up to every machine in the shop again," he said, clearing his throat.

Frasier disconnected the saline drip and swabbed away the drops of blood at the back of his hand from the IV insertion. "You're my only customer today," she responded. "I have to justify them somehow."

"I keep telling you all I really need is some aspirin."

"And I keep telling you you're not twenty-two and immortal anymore, Colonel."

He turned his head to follow her movement around the bed and back to the chair beside him. The movement was too sudden, and he winced and closed his eyes briefly.

"They said you got brushed by an energy beam," she said. "You're very lucky. No broken bones this time, no scrambled internal organs. Just a mild concussion and a case of shock. Dehydrated too, though I don't think that's from whatever hit you. I expect you can probably be out of here in a few hours."

"That means I could get out of here now," he said, but made no effort to throw back the sheet covering him and get out of the bed. "The guy shooting at me probably hit his own feet with his next shot."

"What happened this time?"

"It'll be in the report," he said more or less automatically.

She gave him a stern look. "That's not the deal here, Colonel. I get all the good gossip ahead of time, remember? I have a Need to Know all the latest ways you've found to mess yourselves up so I can keep patching you back together. And I'm not releasing you until you talk."

For an instant a shadow crossed his face, and she regretted her mock threat. Telling Jack O'Neill he was being held prisoner was a stupid joke, stupid and in remarkably poor taste. Apologizing for it would only underline the reason it was particularly inappropriate, and she held her peace and her expression until he relaxed and gave her a wry smile.

"All right, Major. As long as you don't make me sleep."

"Oh?" She raised an elegant eyebrow. "You have something against sleep?"

He sighed. "I think I've done too much sleeping lately. You wouldn't believe what we ran into this time."

"Try me," she said promptly and settled back into the chair like a child waiting for a story.

* * *

"Okay, that *is* a weird one," Janet said thoughtfully nearly an hour later. "I'd love to get my hands on that incense they were burning. It clearly has psychotropic qualities. But that doesn't begin to explain how they found real weapons that you dreamed about. Were they manufacturing them?"

He stared at the ceiling, thinking. "There wasn't time. And I don't know how they could. *We* can't duplicate Goa'uld technology for some of that stuff. How could they?"

"Well, they got them from somewhere. Are you going back to find out? Because if you do, I want to place an order for the incense."

He shook his head, a little less painfully this time. "I don't think so. I want to recommend against it. The whole idea of not knowing whether what you're looking at is real—whether the guy next to you is seeing the same thing or something totally different—it's not . . ." He fell silent. "How do you know what to shoot at?"

"Or whether to shoot at all?" She nodded, understanding. "I guess it's a good thing you didn't dream about some of the really bad stuff, the biochem weapons. Can you imagine letting anthrax loose on your little furry friends? That really *would* wipe them out." She considered. "Or not, I guess. They're probably totally immune to Earth viruses. Although if you could safely eat their food, we've got to have something in common."

"Yeah, that would—" He stopped, and a look of horror crossed his face. "Oh, no. Oh, hell. I've gotta get out of here and talk to Hammond." This time he did throw back the sheet and swing his legs over the side of the bed.

Frasier watched with clinical interest as he supported his weight with his hands, observing the paleness of his face, the slight tremor in his arms. There wasn't much point in telling him to get back to bed at this juncture; his own body would tell him whether he could get up and walk the few steps to the bathroom or closet. Her ace in the hole was knowing where his clothes were.

"About what?" she asked as he caught his breath and prepared to stand up. He was nude, but he was a patient, and he'd been in her care so many times it rarely even occurred to either of them to be self-conscious about it.

"I dreamed about NTS," he said briefly. "I've got to talk to the team. Something Daniel said before we left."

"NTS?" The initials meant nothing to her. That they did to him, and something serious at that, was obvious.

He heaved himself to his feet and swayed a bit. "I'm gonna take a shower," he said, forcing himself to stand still. "When I get out, I want my uniform. Come on, Janet. This is important. Have your wardman page my guys and tell them to meet me in my office in ten minutes."

She considered. "They couldn't come down here and talk to you while you're lying down?"

"No. I've got to report this to Hammond, and I've got to get—" He swayed, cursed again, and muttered an apology.

Whatever those initials stood for, he was seriously worried, and no off-the-shelf medical soothing was going to calm him back into bed. He needed to talk to the boss. "Shower here, so if you get dizzy you can hit the panic button. And come back right after you talk to Hammond so I can make sure you're not just faking it."

"Would I do a thing like that?" he asked, supporting himself on the end of the bed and measuring the distance to the next source of support.

"In a heartbeat, Colonel."

He looked back over his shoulder at her. "I have no secrets from you at all, do I, Major?"

She gave him a long and interested look from the top of his head to the tips of his toes and back. "Not even one, Colonel, and I plan to keep it that way."

He still had the ability to blush, she noted with wicked glee.

*   *   *

On certain rare occasions, the predebriefing meeting that the members of SG-1 regularly held had an air of "let's get our story straight." There was never any actual intent to deceive, but generally the team had to make choices about what they did and did not pass on in their reports. If nothing else, the experience of repeatedly visiting new worlds provided an embarrassment of riches, knowledgewise. Hammond, on the other hand, was notorious for wanting a bottom line.

The bottom line on this one was fuzzy, to say the least.

"Okay, folks, looking for concensus here," O'Neill said, leaning back gingerly in his chair and looking at each of the other three in turn. "Is P4V-837 a world we ought to go back to? Strike off the list entirely? What? Teal'C?"

The Jaffa considered. "If the Goa'uld had visited that world before," he considered, "it seems likely that the Kayeechi would already have the weapons that they . . . appeared . . . to acquire from us, by whatever methods. Since they did not, and their only method of acquiring such weapons appears to be from us, they do not seem to have a great deal to contribute to our battle.

"Besides," he added with a distinctly annoyed expression, "a return to that world would subject us once again to the confusing discrepancies in our perceptions. Those discrepancies could be dangerous. The fact that they were not seriously so this time appears to be a matter of luck."

"I don't know," Jackson said. "When you look at it, they had to have had contact with a number of different cultures in order to produce those different visions of reality. It's as classic a case study in cultural diffusion as you could ask for. I'd love to go back, if there was some way to ensure that I was really seeing what I thought I was seeing."

"They'd only have to pick those images out of our minds," Carter disagreed. "There's nothing that says they'd ever encountered other aliens. Though I really would like to know how they did it," she added. "To be able to manufacture something out of someone's dream—or even see it *in* someone's dream to begin with—suggests an incredible power."

"But it is not a power we can use," Teal'C rumbled. "If we are not Kayeechi, it is inaccessible and useless to us."

"I wonder what the other side in their war is capable of," Daniel mused.

"Does that matter?" Carter asked. She glanced at O'Neill, who was silently listening to the debate, offering no opinion one way or another. She wished the color in his face was a little better; he looked wrung out and worried, as worried as the little purple alien had been back on P4V-837. She started to speak. As she did so, the door to the office opened, and Janet Frasier slipped inside. Jackson immediately rose to offer her his chair, but she shook her head and sat on a low metal file cabinet beside the door.

"Does it matter?" Carter asked again, when the doctor had settled. Her presence made the small office, with its desk and bookcases and posters and wallboards, even more cramped, if possible. It would have been tight with three people. Five was overload. Daniel was sitting with his feet propped up on the rim of the metal wastebasket.

On the other hand, it was a real relief to have Frasier there in case O'Neill fell on his face, which looked like an actual possibility. "They're in the middle of a war. They seemed like nice people— at least up until the end—but we certainly can't trust them. We can't trust anything about that world."

Daniel was insistent. "No, but we can learn from it. I don't know about you, but I saw things in that city that didn't come from my mind. They don't just take weapons. They have art, music, technology—all the things we saw at those celebrations."

"It was illusion," Teal'C declared. "At the end, when we all saw the battlefield"—there was a small pause, during which each of them made some small gesture to indicate that yes, in fact, they *had* all seen a battlefield—"none of the other things, the city, existed."

"I guarantee you that zat gun existed," O'Neill said dryly. "My brains still feel like they've been scrambled. And Janet says the injuries are typical for a near miss."

The team looked to the doctor for confirmation, and she provided it.

"The thing I'm worried about is what *else* they may have taken out of our dreams," O'Neill went on. "How they do it is a subject for the weaponeers. The fact that they manage it is something I will personally attest to. There was no indication before we arrived that they'd ever seen an energy staff, a zat gun, an automatic pistol. Are we agreed on that much?"

They all nodded.

"So we arrive, we have a happy little party, we fall asleep, and we dream. It looks like the Kayeechi have a way to direct the dreaming to some extent. They wanted to know what kind of people we are, and they wanted to put us in scenarios that called for self-defense to see what kind of weapons we're familiar with. Still with me?"

"My dream was about the Book of the Dead," Daniel said thoughtfully. "Especially the part where the heart is weighed against the feather of Ma'at, to see if the Osiris is worthy of the afterlife."

"I thought Osiris was the God of the Dead," Carter said, puzzled.

"It's also the term used to describe the dead person." Daniel leaned forward in his chair, slipping automatically into lecture mode. "In the Book of Going Forth by Day—"

"Hold it," O'Neill interrupted. "We're not in class right now, Professor. The point is that you were tested, right?"

"And Etra'ain said that I sought justice. Ma'at is the symbol of truth. I guess in the context of my focus on Egyptian archaeology, it makes sense that I'd dream that particular ceremony."

"And afterward, you seemed to have actually entered the dreams *we* were having," Carter mused. "Still looking, for truth?"

"I was awake then," Jackson protested. "At least, I'm pretty sure I was." He shuddered suddenly, remembering.

"They take our dreams and make them into reality," Teal'C said uncomfortably.

"No, they couldn't be real," Jackson protested. "I saw all of you dead. I saw *me* dead."

"An alternate reality," Carter suggested. "As if they're trying out the dreams to see which ones fit the best. And then they take the stuff they want, and somehow . . . it becomes real."

"And the stuff they want is weapons." O'Neill

leaned back. "Daniel, did you see anything that indicated they actually understood what they'd gotten from us? That they understood the implications of zat guns and energy staffs even after we showed them what they could do?"

The archaeologist paused, thinking, obviously trying to pick genuine clues to the culture out of the tumble of conflicting, possibly illusory impressions of P4V-837. "Not really," he said. "I wish I could go back and . . ." He looked up and smiled briefly at the looks of distaste on the faces of his teammates. "Well, you know what I mean. Based on the foods we ate, and the fact that we were actually housed in a cave, I almost think that their culture is technologically *very* primitive, maybe just above the hunter-gatherer stage in fact. The only processed food I remember is bread, and it wasn't highly refined bread. The utensils were relatively simple. They seemed to rely on us for the more sophisticated images of what we saw, but they didn't really know how to make use of it. Otherwise maybe we'd have been sleeping in a basic hotel room instead of the cave."

"Maybe they just couldn't make an entire city zap into existence that fast," Carter said. "The weapons were relatively small." She shook her head. "But you said you were here, Daniel. That's pretty large scale."

"So was the coral city and your island," O'Neill pointed out.

Carter shook her head. "I keep remembering this little thing called the Law of Conservation of Energy, and I want to know how they could take a *dream* and turn it into something *real* you could shoot somebody with. They've created an entire culture based on imagination and too many baked beans. It's impossible."

"Oh, I wouldn't say that," O'Neill contradicted. He spun his chair around—there was just room behind the desk to do it—and stared at the poster of the galaxy on the back wall of the office. "They managed somehow. They really did reach into our dreams and come out with real weapons. And that's what bothers me. I'd hate to think that we were responsible for obliterating their entire world."

"With a couple of zat guns?" Jackson asked, surprised. "I mean, surely they can't maintain them without us there to keep dreaming for them. They may have weapons, but they don't have the means to even keep them clean. They don't even know they have to."

"I'm not talking about zat guns." O'Neill's chair squeaked as he came back forward and swung around to face them. "I'm talking about full-blown thermonuclear bombs."

CHAPTER THIRTEEN

At three o'clock in the afternoon, SG-1 assembled for its formal mission debriefing in the glass-walled room overlooking the Gate. They were unusually subdued, George Hammond thought as he came in the door. No joking or small talk or heated discussion this time. Just the soft shuffling of papers being looked over one last time, the clinking of ice in the water pitcher.

"Be seated," he said as the team rose automatically at his entrance. He took his place at the head of the table and looked down its length.

Janet Frasier had remained standing. "Sir."

"Yes, Major?"

"Request permission to remain for the briefing."

"Certainly, Major."

The formalities having been observed, Frasier

sat down again across from Major Carter, diagonally from O'Neill.

Interesting, Hammond thought and took another look at the team leader.

Frasier wouldn't have permitted O'Neill to be here if she didn't think he was up to it, but there were circles under his eyes and the water pitcher trembled a tattoo against the glass as he poured. He set the pitcher down again a little more sharply than necessary and took a deep breath.

One of these days, son, you're going to find out you have limits, Hammond thought.

The other members of the team looked tired too, but not as exhausted, and they didn't move as if they remembered a time when every bone hurt. They sat back in their chairs and waited for the colonel to speak.

O'Neill took a swallow of the water and cleared his throat. "Our mission objective was to perform reconnaissance, determine threats, and if possible make peaceful contact with the inhabitants, if any, of the planet designated P4V-837." He stared down at the piece of paper in his hands for a moment as if he'd forgotten what it was for. "I think we failed." He sounded doubtful.

"Stealing dreams is certainly one way to win an arms race," George Hammond said. He'd heard a lot of bizarre stories in his time, but this one was in the running for top ten, at least for this week. "Can we use the Kayeechi's ability against the Goa'uld?"

"That would presuppose the Kayeechi would be willing to ally with us," Jackson answered. "I didn't see any sign they wanted allies. Only weapons. And if they haven't encountered the Goa'uld yet, why should they get into our war? They have a war of their own to fight."

"And if they can pull bombs out the same way they could zat guns, there may not be anything left of them to help us anyway," Carter added.

"But all you saw was a bright light. Maybe they don't have a bomb out of your dream. Maybe you're just Thomas Edison." Hammond was arguing both sides with equal facility, forcing his people to consider all the possibilities.

Frasier was listening quietly to the conversational flow, which darted back and forth like leaves in churned water. Once the summary had been made, the debate about what had really happened was open. It was difficult to tell who was on which side, however.

"Unfortunately, sir, if it's true, this particular dream has the potential to destroy everything on that world," O'Neill pointed out. "If they could create a zat gun out of absolutely nothing, there's no reason they couldn't create a high-yield nuclear bomb the same way."

"I'm finding this very difficult to believe," Hammond said. "I know we talk about dreaming things up, but usually it takes billions of dollars to do it. You're talking about cutting a lot of corners in R&D."

O'Neill sighed. "Sir, I don't really believe it either. But I saw the guns. I was *shot* at. You know how convincing that can be."

"Unless your first guess about an arms cache was correct," Hammond pointed out. "They could have had access to the guns all along."

"I'd like to think that was the case. But I don't believe it. Honestly, sir, I don't know what to believe. But I know what I'm afraid of."

"Telepathy and telekinesis maybe?" Jackson speculated. "It's a big universe out there."

Hammond thought about it for a few very long minutes, weighing the possibility that his primary team had completely lost all their marbles versus their so far extremely respectable track record. Jackson was right: It *was* a big universe out there. "Very well. Your recommendation, Colonel?"

O'Neill closed his eyes, took a deep breath, and let it out again. "My recommendation is twofold, sir.

"Our mission calls for peaceful contact. We

may have inadvertently provided the natives, who may be mentally highly advanced but technologically are not, with a weapon far beyond their capability to handle wisely. I believe we have a responsibility to undo that damage if we can. That's the first thing.

"The second thing is that once that's done, we shut the door and never go back there."

Hammond scanned the rest of the team. They seemed to be in agreement; at least no one was making faces or muttering to him- or herself.

"Are you sure they're not technologically advanced?" he asked, just to be sure. "Could they have had cities floating in the sky like the Nox, somewhere you couldn't see them?"

"I don't believe so, sir. Everything we saw was consistent with a low-tech culture." Jackson was definite on that point. "As for the bomb, well, maybe it wouldn't destroy everything on that world. Just everything we know about." At the look O'Neill shot him, Jackson went on. "We don't know anything about what could be on the next continent over, Jack. I'm just saying that there could be a very highly organized technological culture on the other side of the planet, and we just landed—"

"In Wonderland? I doubt it. The Gates tend to show up in proximity to the most developed culture on the planet, at least for the time they're built. Whether you want to argue cause or effect there—"

"It is true," Teal'C confirmed. "The Goa'uld assume that the civilizations nearest the Gate will reflect the greatest advancement on the planet."

"But didn't we have a Gate in Egypt? And Iceland?" Carter shivered at the memory and glanced at O'Neill.

"The Goa'uld are not always correct," Teal'C said dryly.

"At the time the Gate was set in place there, Egypt *was* among the most highly advanced cultures on Earth. We don't know whether there might have been one in China too, of course, but—"

"All right, that's enough," Hammond snapped, bringing the flat of his hand down on the table. He had seen enough late-night bull sessions to recognize one when it took wing at his own conference table. "The bottom line, Colonel. Is there any reason—does *Earth* have any reason—to expend further materiel and budget, not to mention personnel, on P4V-837?"

Jackson and Carter subsided, looking guilty. Carter reached for the pitcher and poured a glass of water for herself and Frasier. Jackson shoved a glass her way, and after a moment, she filled one for him too.

O'Neill took a deep breath and answered Hammond's question. "Only if we want to assume P4V-837 will go on existing, sir. Nuclear weapons are more than they could have possibly bargained for. I don't want to take responsibility for that particular nightmare. It's like—" He searched for an analogy, and his face hardened in remembered pain. "It's like giving a kid a gun without telling them what it is, sir. I don't want to live with that."

"But you can't control your dreams, and neither can they," Hammond objected. "And they had to ask you to show them how to use the zat guns and energy staff. If you just dreamed a test, they couldn't get anything useful out of that. Could they?"

O'Neill thought back over the dream, over what he had remembered from classified lectures as he watched the bomb, trailing its wires, being set into its cradle, and remembered Vair, watching his every movement, his every expression.

"I think I dreamed enough," O'Neill said bleakly. "I know I was thinking about how the bomb was inert on the test tower, and then I was in the control room when they set it off. All they'd know is the destruction. They wouldn't know anything about the radiation or just *how much* power we're talking about. If they set off the real thing, it'll wipe out their neighbors, but it'll take them out too. And probably most of the immediate surroundings for the next ten thousand years or so."

The six people seated around the table contemplated that possibility. Even Hammond closed his eyes to repudiate the horror of it; it was one thing to have such things as a deterrence against an enemy who had them too for the same reason. It was something else entirely to jump from stone axes to radioactive ruins literally overnight. And he still wasn't convinced it was even possible.

"You seem awfully certain that they'd be willing to use such a weapon, Colonel. Perhaps they've got more sense than we do."

"The Kayeechi would use any weapon they believed would give them victory," Teal'C said. "They are desperate. They believed they are fighting for their survival. They may be right. Given the opportunity to strike a mortal blow to their enemy, they will do so."

"And to themselves in the process," O'Neill said softly. "But they don't know that."

Hammond bit his lip. Then he said slowly, "But if all they saw was a bright light, Colonel, why would they assume that it was a weapon? And how could they make the translation between a 'bright light' and a functional bomb?"

There was a small silence around the table. Then O'Neill cleared his throat. "There was more than a bright light, sir. If they were seeing my dream, they actually saw a unit on a test tower. They saw the triggering mechanism. And they'd know it was a weapon from my reaction. I don't think it will take the Kayeechi long to put together their own nuclear test, even if they only recreate what they saw through my eyes. Remember, they created functional zat guns and energy staffs from nothing more than that.

"They've got the potential for a bomb. I don't know how they did it, but they took it from my mind. I gave it to them."

Hammond started to respond. Before he could speak, however, Daniel jumped in again. It wasn't entirely clear whether he was trying to provide a counterargument to the proposal or just offer some comfort to O'Neill.

"Okay, so they got it out of your dream, but that doesn't make you responsible for it. It was a nightmare, after all. Jack, you can't be blamed for this. You can't control dreams. And it's not your fault you know what you know." Jackson was repeating himself, trying to convince the other man. It wasn't working.

It did provide an opportunity to interrupt, however, and the general took it. "Even given the possibility that you're right, Colonel, how would you propose to undo what you've done? It seems that horse is out of the barn."

O'Neill started to answer then stopped. "I was thinking I could undream it," he said at last. "But we don't have the ability the natives have—we think they have—to do whatever it is they do. They're as far beyond us in that area as we are beyond them in hardware."

"But you *can* control dreams," Frasier interrupted thoughtfully. The others at the table jumped, startled to realize they'd forgotten her presence. She looked up, slightly embarrassed. When she realized they were all looking at her, waiting for her to go on, she did so, with growing confidence. "Or at least, some people claim you can. And it might go along with the 'triggering' you mentioned, Dr. Jackson. And isn't that exactly what you said the aliens were doing? 'They made you dream it.' "

"Major, would you care to elucidate?" Hammond was grateful for the change in vector. The discussion was getting tangled up in who was to blame, and that wasn't the issue. He wasn't absolutely sure the issue had been identified yet. Maybe Frasier could clarify matters.

"On our world, it's called dream awareness. Some people call it 'lucid dreaming.' You're asleep, you're dreaming, but you're aware of the fact, and you can actually control what happens in the dream—your own actions and even the actions of others."

"You're rigging a dice game with Morpheus," Jackson murmured. "Using loaded dice."

"Go on, Doctor." Hammond leaned forward, his interest piqued. "Do you mean human beings may have something like the . . . *ability* of these aliens?"

"Well, sir, over a hundred years ago a man named van Eeden wrote about awareness of dreaming while actually in the dream state. Since then, it's become well known that stimulation of certain centers in the brain with different chemicals, lights, or even sounds can result in very different kinds of dreams: good dreams, nightmares, even dreams with consistent kinds of results. I've seen a study that showed some people responded to certain kinds of allergy medication. In those individuals the medication stimulates certain brain centers. They'd have nightmares, but nightmares where the dreamer always triumphed. It affected a very particular area of the brain in a very specific way.

"Studies of people in the dream-awareness state show that they tend to exhibit characteristic brain patterns. People can be trained to reach that mental state through biofeedback. Or it can be"—she hesitated, then went on with distaste—"induced for short periods."

"Oh my. That's amazing," Carter said excitedly. "I've heard people claim they knew they were dreaming when they were having a nightmare and were trying to wake up from it. But I've never heard they could direct the dream."

"Controlled dreaming? Sounds like a dream come true," O'Neill waxed ironic.

"Theoretically," Frasier answered. "Or really, more than theoretical."

"There's a certain aspect of danger in it too, of course. Freud said that our minds preserve memories and emotions we may not remember consciously. Emotions we can't deal with easily are disguised in our dreams as other things. You don't know what you might dredge up in that arena."

"I never had dreams like that," Teal'C muttered.

Jackson shot him an extremely skeptical look.

"Well, we don't know enough about your brain," Frasier said to the Jaffa apologetically. "Or how your symbiote might affect those particular kinds of mental states. But we have some idea about our own. And about the dreaming techniques. It's been done in the laboratory, at least. The success rate isn't a hundred percent by any means, but some amazing things have been reported."

"So we could use this technique, maybe induce it with some kind of cerebral stimulation, and have a pretty good chance of undoing what we did?" Carter asked.

"What I did," O'Neill corrected her. "Then we have to. I can't inflict nuclear weaponry on a culture that's not ready for it. I have a responsibility to those people."

"Wait just one minute, people," Hammond said. "You're talking about messing around with the brains of my people, Doctor, and I'm not willing to take that risk. This sounds extremely chancy. And I suppose it would take some time to learn this technique you're talking about. You don't do this sort of thing overnight. If Colonel O'Neill is right, it may be too late already."

"But, sir," Jackson said, "maybe it isn't too late, either. And if it isn't, we can't just let them take a weapon like that out of Jack's mind and let them totally destroy themselves. If there's a chance we can undo that damage, or prevent it from ever happening, we have to try. We have a moral obligation."

The two men—young archaeologist and weathered general—faced each other over the table eye to eye.

"I have a *moral obligation* to protect my world," Hammond said at last. "That doesn't include throwing away my best resources to correct a mistake that might not even be real."

"Hey, was that a compliment?" O'Neill asked the room at large. The comment escaped from him unintentionally, falling into a sudden pool of silence at the table. He winced as he realized they'd all heard it.

Hammond glared at him. "It's a realistic assessment of your value to this program, Colonel, and don't you forget it. I don't do *compliments*."

"Yes, sir," O'Neill said innocently. "Of course not, sir."

Hammond gave him a beady glare. O'Neill decided that shutting up was the better part of valor, at least for the moment.

Jackson wasn't giving up. "Sir, part of our value lies in our willingness to take risks, explore—"

"Strange new worlds," O'Neill put in. "New civilizations." This whole conversation had taken on an air of unreality for him, as if he were back dreaming on P4V-837 again. He could no more repress his responses than he could stop breathing.

Jackson, along with the rest of them, ignored him. Even Hammond pretended he couldn't hear. "This is a new area with considerable potential for gain, sir. As for risk, well, every time we step through the Gate we're taking a risk. Why should this be any different?"

"All we'd have to do is go back, get some of that incense stuff, bring it back, and try it out here under controlled conditions," Carter said with rising excitement. "We can see if we can manipulate our own surroundings right here at the Complex! Maybe it's not just something on P4V-837. Maybe it's something we can actually use against the Goa'uld!"

"Absolutely not!" O'Neill said before Hammond had a chance to open his mouth. "I'm not going to turn whaddayacall'em—Morpheus— loose in the Complex. Especially not when Janet's been talking about biochemical weapons, and thank you so much for planting *that* suggestion, I might add. What if I start dreaming about *that* instead of solving the problem?"

"We'll just have to come along and make sure you don't," Jackson said determinedly. "You're not going to do this alone, you know."

"Am I talking to myself here?" Hammond asked rhetorically with an air of finally getting a word in edgewise. "I thought I vetoed this idea."

"No, sir, you aren't, and you haven't yet, but I think this is a way for us to help Jack *and* undo the damage *and* fulfill our primary mission to obtain new technology and weapons against the

Goa'uld. You've got to give us the chance, General. Please." Jackson had applied all the earnestness he had to his argument. It was a considerable amount.

The team held its breath.

Hammond was wavering.

"It's my duty, sir," O'Neill said softly into another pool of silence. He met Hammond's gaze across the broad table. "Daniel's been doing my talking for me, but it's something I have to do. I have to try, at least. You understand that."

Rather than answering his subordinate directly, Hammond shifted focus to his medical expert. "Doctor Frasier, does this have a hope in hell of working?" the general asked. "And what is the risk to Colonel O'Neill if he tries it?"

Frasier, finding herself on the hot seat, swallowed and said, "Yes, sir. I think it does. There are certain mechanical learning techniques we can combine with biofeedback training to help speed the process, and we can artificially maintain the necessary electrical activity level in the brain. I think it's possible. There really shouldn't be any risk, except—"

"Except what?"

"Well, sir, the part we don't know about is how the Kayeechi turn dreams into reality. Normally, what you experience in the dream state is just imagination, a mental construct if you will.

But in this case we have some evidence that what happens in the dream reality actually is, er, real. Dr. Jackson says he bit his lip."

"And it still hurts," he supplied, probing the raw place.

"He might have done that while he slept. But that doesn't explain the smell of liquor the rest of the team detected on him after his last walk through the dream world."

Jackson shuddered suddenly, seeing an overlay of this same room in ruins with Hammond lying dead. He shook his head hard to make the vision go away. "It sure tasted real."

"So I can't say there is no risk at all, sir. I just don't have any idea how to measure it. But I believe we can do it, yes."

"Artificially maintain?" O'Neill was still back on methodology. It was his turn to swallow nervously, but he nodded. "There you have it, General. Piece of cake."

CHAPTER FOURTEEN

Hammond snorted. "You think I haven't heard that one before, Colonel?" He paused, thinking, weighing alternatives, while the team and the chief medical officer watched him eagerly.

It was Hammond's responsibility, ultimately, and while he abhorred the picture Jack and Daniel had painted, he still wasn't entirely convinced. The proposed solution seemed almost as outlandish as the problem. If it had been anyone other than Janet Frasier suggesting it, he would have dismissed the whole thing out of hand and sent the originator of the idea to the chief medical officer for a mental examination. But Frasier couldn't very well perform a mental examination on herself, and she seemed certain that there was something to this nonsense.

Still, it *was* nonsense. "I know you like to fly by the seat of your pants on these missions, Colonel, and given that you have no idea what to expect out there, I normally have no objection. But for this one I'd like to see something more like a plan—always assuming it works to begin with.

"For one thing, exactly how do you propose to accomplish this little feat of altruism? We're not talking about time travel here. The damage has been done, as you've already pointed out. We've been trying to put that cat back into the bag for half a century and can't do it. What makes you think you can dream up a solution for the Kay-eechi?"

The pun was deliberate and delivered mostly for the pleasure of seeing the look on O'Neill's face. The colonel seemed to think he had a lock on smart remarks, and it didn't hurt to remind him he could be outranked in that category too.

But meanwhile, the general had moved beyond a flat no. Carter, always willing to argue, was more than happy to seize the opportunity.

"Sir, if you'll recall, Daniel was able to enter their dream realities when he was awake and we were asleep. He actually interacted—well, almost—with them. The aliens *did* interact with all of us, in all our dreams. That supports what Janet's saying.

"So why can't we do the same? What if we let Colonel O'Neill dream a second nuclear test, one that absolutely *fails*, one where the explosion doesn't happen or something else goes badly wrong? That should be enough to keep the Kay-eechi from trying to use the weapon.

"They don't actually know enough about the mechanics to fix a bomb, sir. All they'd be left with is something that doesn't work. They won't even know why, so they can't experiment with it. The three of us can help him out, be there to support him, even wake him up if things go bad. Dr. Frasier can get her samples and new data. It's an acceptable risk, sir." At the look on Hammond's face, she added quietly, "It's worth a try, considering the alternatives."

Hammond looked from one member of the team to the next, measuring the commitment in their eyes. "What guarantees do you have that you won't all be affected the same way you were the first time?" he asked at last. "How do you know you wouldn't just be dreaming you were doing all this?"

That stopped them for the moment. They traded glances around the long table. Then O'Neill said slowly, "Well, that might happen. But if all of us experience the same thing and it turns out to only be a dream, well, at least we'll have done our best as far as we could. That's another reason why we'd need all of us, sir: to provide perspective."

"I can give them filters, General," Janet said.

"We've got the experimental ones that they're working on to replace gas masks—small enough to fit inside the nostrils so they won't be noticed. If it's really the incense triggering the dream sequences, that should keep them from being affected." The medical officer was nodding, certain of herself. "I can run some tests to see if there are any residual effects in their blood. I got a sample from the Colonel, of course, but I can test the others too. Maybe it's just a matter of the right antihistamine."

"Again," muttered Jackson sourly. He'd had enough of histamine effects on a previous mission. His chronic allergies, mild though they were, usually kept him protected from alien pollens, but the results when he didn't take them had proved to be problematic, to say the least. "What if we need the incense in order to make the dreams real though? Maybe that's important to the whole Kayeechi process. It wouldn't do any good for Jack to bollix up the bomb if *his* bomb is only a dream and *their* bomb is the real thing."

"We just answered that one, Daniel."

Daniel removed his glasses and pinched the bridge of his nose. "You did?" He thought over the last few minutes' conversation. "Oh. I guess you did. Well, then, all Jack needs to do is sabotage the test one way or the other. Simple. Right?"

Meanwhile, O'Neill was thinking through the details of the problem, trying out mental scenarios. Now that saving the Kayeechi from their own potential looked like a possibility, Hammond's question was to the point, and Daniel had put his finger on one of the problems. "Daniel, what makes you think *I* know enough about the mechanics of a bomb to keep one from triggering?" O'Neill said.

Jackson gave him a wry look. "You don't have to either confirm or deny it. Although I'm betting you know at least as much as I do, and anyone in freshman physics knows what a critical mass is.

"But all you have to do is show that it doesn't work. To keep it from working, that is. That should be enough to stop them. And you probably can think of a few dozen snafus that have stopped tests." When O'Neill opened his mouth, Jackson raised his hand. "I don't know and I don't care and it's probably classified beyond belief anyway. It doesn't matter. All you have to do is dream a test that doesn't work. Simple."

"Simple, he says." O'Neill was still waxing ironic. "And if I don't? Suppose I try to do something like that, and instead of failing, the bomb goes off in my dream. Will it go off in real life too? And if it does, what happens to us? Being ground zero is not my goal in life, Daniel."

"Blowing up an innocent culture isn't your goal in life either, is it?" Jackson wasn't playing the game.

A chilly silence fell across the conference table.

"That's nasty, Daniel," the colonel said evenly.

"I learned from the best," the younger man said, just as evenly.

Frasier and Carter exchanged a private rolling-eyed glance. Teal'C frowned. Hammond gave a little sigh.

"And what if General Hammond is right and they've already used the bomb?"

"We'll send a probe through first. Once they see us, they'll probably concentrate on trying to pick our brains some more. We won't tell them we know what they're up to."

"How would you explain your return?" Hammond asked, moving toward capitulation without committing himself.

"We could say . . ." Daniel floundered. "Uh, well . . ."

"We could say we left my eyeliner behind and we've got to get it," Carter said. At the incredulous looks from the rest of them, she went on. "Well why not? It's not like they're going to know the difference. It could be a ritual religious object, for all they know."

"All right," Hammond said at last, breaking the silence as they contemplated the idea. "If you really think this has a chance to work, Doctor, and they have a chance to get what you need—"

"I'll have to go with them," Frasier said gently.

"Absolutely not," Hammond and O'Neill said at the same time. The colonel glanced at the general and decided to let him issue the orders.

"You may *not* go," Hammond said. "You haven't had the experience, and you're too valuable here."

"Without me it won't work," she responded. "Lucid dreaming requires that the brain remain in a beta state for extended periods. If you haven't practiced, it won't happen. I can induce that state artificially with a cerebral stimulator— I think." The last two words had a tinge of doubt, but then she lifted her chin. "If I don't go, sir, they might as well stay home, and millions of Kayeechi, not to mention those other aliens, the octopus ones, will die."

"Well, maybe not millions," Jackson said sotto voce. "Thousands maybe. Depending on population densities."

She ignored him. "Besides, my being on the scene will ensure that Colonel O'Neill will avoid any negative effects from combining the alien drugs with the recent shock to his system from the zat gun."

Hammond let go an explosive, exasperated breath and drummed his fingers on the conference table. "I am *not* happy about this, people," he warned them. "On the other hand, it's not our purpose to spread death and destruction throughout the galaxy."

"I agree," Teal'C said unexpectedly. "That is the purpose of the Goa'uld."

Hammond, who hadn't finished his thought, glared at the Jaffa. "Nor is it our purpose to risk our personnel unnecessarily. *Therefore*," he said pointedly, "I will allow you to attempt this ... real-life thought experiment under two conditions. One: Before any return to Kayeechi to try it, Col. O'Neill and Dr. Frasier will demonstrate in the laboratory that this 'lucid dreaming' concept actually works. And two: if you do establish that it works, you may make one attempt on the planet with the understanding that this will be the *only* such attempt.

"Furthermore," he continued grimly, "if Dr. Frasier is going to go, I want Teal'C and Dr. Jackson to remain here." At the incipient eruption of protest, he raised one hand. "I heard what you said about needing all of you to provide perspective. I think that the three of you, particularly Dr. Frasier, can meet that goal. So only the three of you. And I am giving each one of you a direct order, Colonel, ladies. If you do go, come back in one piece. And when you do, we are going to shut the door to P4V-837 permanently."

Dumbfounded, the other five people at the table stared at their commanding officer. Then, carefully choosing his words, O'Neill inquired, "Sir, permission to ask a question."

Hammond's lips tightened. "Permission granted."

"Why split the team?"

"Because if this dream technique works, Colonel, but you don't come back from this mission of mercy and manage to cost me two more good officers in the process, I want someone here who has had the experience with this world to help us recognize the next one like it we run across. I'm not going to debate this, Colonel. You have your orders."

Daniel opened his mouth to protest. Under Hammond's glare, he shut it again. A moment later, Hammond stood, signaling that the briefing was over, and everyone else at the table rose as well, keeping silent until he had left the conference room.

"This isn't fair," Jackson said to the closed door.

"This is the military, Daniel," O'Neill informed him gently. "It isn't supposed to be fair."

"But this is crazy! We're a team!"

"And he's a general. We might not like it, but we've got our orders." O'Neill gathered together the briefing packet scattered on the table before him and tapped them into a neat stack. "So let's get started."

"What are *we* supposed to do while they're out there?" a still rebellious Jackson demanded of Teal'C.

Teal'C looked back at him impassively. "Wait. It is what armies do."

CHAPTER FIFTEEN

As they made their way back to the infirmary a few minutes later, a slightly stunned Frasier dropped back to ask Carter, "Aren't you always supposed to come back in one piece?"

"It's nice, but it's not the top priority," O'Neill answered, overhearing her. "How long will it take you to get packed up and ready to go, Doctor?"

She laughed despite herself. "Don't we have orders to try the technique out first, Colonel? You never know. A little practice might do us both some good."

"Oh, well if you think we need to *practice*," he said.

"I want to take some time to review the materials on lucid dreaming," she said. "And there are some things I want to get together."

O'Neill paused, causing a small traffic jam in the hallway as the rest of the team crowded around and blocked the passage of several Gate technicians going off shift. "I gather that this waking-while-you're-sleeping technique isn't exactly restful."

"Not necessarily," Frasier acknowledged.

"All right, we can use the extra time to get our own game plan together. Teal'C—"

"We shall prepare a probe to gather more data at P4V-837," Teal'C said seriously. Carter nodded.

"Make sure to put some roc repellant on it," O'Neill said. Frasier, confused, just shook her head. Some things medical personnel were not meant to understand.

"I'll go look at tapes and try to put some guesses together about what the Kayeechi culture is really like," Daniel said.

"You'll excuse me," O'Neill continued. "I think I'm going to go take a nice, clean, dream-free afternoon nap. If you're right, Doctor, I'm going to need my beauty sleep."

"I don't know how you can stand to," Jackson muttered.

"Gotta face it sometime."

While the rest of the team scattered, O'Neill continued with Frasier back to the infirmary. He seemed more than willing to lie back down on the hospital bed, though, Frasier noticed, though he eyed her bustling around the room rather sus-piciously. "What's that stuff?" He was, whether he wanted to admit it or not, still feeling the ef-fects of that near miss. It worried her.

"Just a few basics," she said with a profes-sional soothe in her voice. "Go ahead and get some rest, Colonel. I've got some reading to do, and you're not fully recovered yet anyway. Just take the boots off, will you? Those are clean sheets."

"Women. Never happy," he muttered with a small grin. He sat on the edge of the bed to un-lace and remove the heavy black combat boots. Once they were off, he swung his legs back up and wiggled his toes inside his socks, sighing with contentment.

"Nose filters, right. Thanks for the reminder, Colonel." Frasier smiled back at him and ducked out of the ward for her office, where she promptly turned on the camera monitor to watch her sole patient.

He didn't seem apprehensive about falling asleep at least. No traumatic insomnia. It re-mained to be seen whether he would wake up with the cold sweats.

One hand behind his head and the other flung across his chest, he stared up at the ceiling tiles for a few minutes and sighed again. As she watched, his eyes gradually closed, his head fell to one side, and the arm across his chest slipped down to rest on the sheet beside him. His breathing slowed and deepened. A good soldier could fall asleep anywhere, anytime, the body grabbing whatever rest was available in order to be prepared to meet the next onslaught. O'Neill had that technique, at least, down pat. And his face, laugh lines smoothed away in rest, showed no signs of distress.

"Good," she whispered and sat down to do some fast cramming on the subject of lucid dreaming. She clicked on the computer keyboard, making the shifting-lines screensaver disappear, and entered her password to access the Net. Besides the plethora of ordinary Web sites on lucid dreaming, she was fairly sure that she could find solid information in military studies normally unavailable to the average physician. The military was always interested in the human mind. If they had a project to develop telepathy or "distant viewing," she was morally certain there would be something in the records about dreaming, lucid, induction of the state thereof.

She was glad this one wasn't going to be turned over to the research teams. It wasn't often she got to do her own datamining, and she delighted in the opportunity. While the wardroom monitor flickered over her head, she focused on her computer screen, ignoring the still figure on the bed.

Meanwhile, in the sterile quiet of the ward room, Jack O'Neill was slipping through layers and levels of sleep, sliding deeper, until beneath his eyelids his eyes flickered, watching the images formed in his brain as once again he began to dream.

But his eyes remained closed; so there was no one to see when a small figure appeared next to him, a small figure with an odd pattern of red hair growing in neat symmetrical lines across its skin and only three fingers on each hand. Vair was dressed in a coarse undyed tunic that came to his knees, and on the rope belt around his waist he carried a badly forged metal knife, its handle wrapped in a thin cord woven of plant fibers.

The little alien looked around the room with fascination, awed at the rough wool fabric of the blanket and the smooth, impervious hardness of the desk built into the wall. He tried poking gingerly at the shiny pole of the IV tree and biting it experimentally. When the metal remained unmarred, he looked at the man on the bed.

"See, Etra'ain," he murmured. "You are not the only one who can walk and Shape in the minds of others."

Jack stirred uneasily in his sleep. Vair jumped,

startled, and then addressed him directly. "Listen to me, Tall One. We need you with us. We need you to show us how to cause the great lightning. You have to come back with me, come back to Kayeechi. You have to help me show Etra'ain that I have as much power as she does. Unless—Do you have more weapons here that can save us, that I can take?"

But Jack O'Neill was sleeping and made no answer.

Instead, the small red-furred humanoid stepped out the door and out of the range of the security camera that monitored the sickbed, venturing into the very heart of the Stargate Complex.

Security rests upon three legs: detect the intruder, delay his access to the target, and intercept him.

Like any tripod, this is inherently unstable. Rather than depend on mere human perceptions, technology has developed highly sensitive methods for identifying intruders and delights in creating ever more imaginative ways to make it difficult to reach what it seeks to protect.

In the long run, however, interception always involves a mere human.

But how can technology detect a dream? And how can it delay access when the intruder is within the target to begin with?

Vair was finding the Stargate Complex utterly fascinating. While the Security Communications staff charged with monitoring the monitors blinked and shook their collective heads, certain they must have dozed off for a moment—that little red fuzzy thing wasn't on the tape, so it must have been too much chile for lunch—the little alien was roaming through, first, the infirmary, and then into the rest of the complex.

The Tall Ones had strong dreams, he was finding. Etra'ain should come and see—but no. Why add to her power when he could keep all this for himself? This place was full of Tall Ones, but it was also full of little rooms and odd corridors, and if he thought about it, he could keep himself out of the awake ones' dreaming. There was no reason for them to see what they did not expect to see.

Of course, it was difficult sometimes to concentrate on such a thing when there were so many other things to look at. Boxes everywhere of metal harder than his knife and dark glass that sometimes lit up and showed images almost like dreams. He poked at one such, trying to make it follow his shaping, but it ignored him and went on doing what it wished instead. It was the box itself that made the images, he realized at last, and that frightened him. Inanimate objects were not supposed to be able to Shape. What kind of world was this?

But there were a number of other things about this world that were worthy of remembering for the future. That raised, hard surface, for example, supported by side panels—that would be good for keeping food clean. Those little sticks that lay everywhere made marks; there might be some use for those too, though he couldn't imagine what.

Looking into the sleeping man, he tried to understand what the little sticks were for. But he could not reach in as easily as before; he could see that they were not weapons, and for the time being, that was enough.

There were little knobs in the walls at regular intervals, and he tugged on them to see what would happen. Sometimes nothing at all; sometimes the wall came away, swinging wide to reveal cabinets or more rooms. One such was stacked from floor to ceiling with thin transparent skins that held row upon row of soft white cylinders. He tried to pick one up, but it was too large for his hand to hold. Moments later the entire pile fell on him, bouncing off his head and body and landing in awkward piles all over the little room, sliding into the hallway as well. Vair scampered away, panicking, and ran down the hallway, dashing in between the Tall Ones who

looked startled and shook their heads and sometimes took glass things off of their faces and polished them frantically.

Weapons. He needed weapons, but he had no
idea whether what he saw were weapons or not.
He could not make these Tall Ones shape to his
command; he had no *mor'ee-rai*. Merely the ability to follow the Tall One to his home would not
impress the Circle. He needed to bring back
something spectacular, something that would
destroy the Narrai and force Etra'ain and the
Kayeechi to recognize him as important.

Meanwhile, Jack O'Neill dreamed on, an annoyed expression twisting his handsome features as the Kayeechi aliens persisted in showing
up in the oddest places.

Janet Frasier sat back from her computer
screen and sighed. It was all very well to connect
a vague memory of cerebral stimulation with the
various stages of sleep, but maintaining the right
level of activity for a lengthy period of time—at
least hours, she suspected, if not days—without
burning out either the equipment or the brain involved was a tricky proposition. The literature
said that the human brain didn't particularly
enjoy being forced to remain in a single sleep
stage for a prolonged period of time. Fully realized, vivid dreams could last mere moments.

The literature described planned dreams: sex,

gambling, thrills that the waking subject would never have sought out, thrills made safe by the fact that they were only dreams, and while scientists could say definitively that a person was dreaming, no one could tell the actual content of the dream but the dreamer himself. This led to the unnerving possibility that the whole subject of "lucid" dreaming was nothing more than the subjects' fantasy, since there was no objective verification possible. Maybe the reports were just vivid imagination, and she was wasting her time.

"And down that road madness lies," Frasier told herself. She wasn't going to allow herself to be drawn into a Moebius strip of arguments trying to prove something that simply didn't lend itself to the scientific method.

Still, the literature did specify the type and frequency of stimulation most often associated with self-reported successful lucid dreaming. And she could, in fact, jury-rig such stimulation without much difficulty. She began making notes in a careful, precise hand, listing everything she thought she needed.

Elsewhere in the complex, Daniel Jackson and Teal'C were examining the probe data from the latest venture into P4V-837. The data transmitted back from the brave little machine showed that the planet was still, for the moment at least, in one piece; radiation levels were still consistent with normal background counts for a planet with two suns and not much in the way of heavy metals. The two of them watched, fascinated, as a shadow slid over the probe, and something yanked it up from the ground. For several dizzying moments they got a wildly swaying view of the horizon, the forest, and something that might have been feathers before the probe ceased transmitting.

"Could that have been another roc?" Jackson asked of no one in particular.

Teal'C, who was the only other person present in the small conference room they had commandeered for their work, and who had a tendency to be literal-minded, chose to respond. "It is entirely possible. The creature we saw was certainly large enough to take the probe. Although I still do not understand how it can fly. It is too large for that wingspan to be aerodynamically efficient."

"I don't suppose it matters in the long run," the archaeologist said. "Though if they took that probe deliberately, they may be intelligent. I'd love to study them. Imagine an intelligent avian society!"

"I am sure it would be interesting," Teal'C responded politely. He could not possibly care less about avian societies. The truly interesting point, as far as he was concerned, was that the probe had given them no indications of any recent thermonuclear detonations on P4V-837.

"I guess we have what we need for the time being anyway." Daniel blinked and shook his head. He was used to Teal'C's sturdy pragmatism. While the Jaffa was willing to humor his human friends on many things, if a topic wasn't related to the eventual defeat of the Goa'uld and the freeing of their Jaffa slaves, it would never be truly important in Teal'C's eyes. "I think I'm going to take a nap myself before Janet tries out her theory on Jack. I'm so tired I'm seeing things. Without, please God, any dreams at all. I really, really don't want to 'see things' anymore for a long, long time." He took a deep breath and let it out slowly, reminding himself that this room was *not* filled with stinking corpses and he was *not* being followed around by a little red-furred alien.

It had taken a while for it to dawn on Vair that this place was the same that the Tall One had shaped in his dream. It looked very different, of course: no signs of death and decay, no bodies sprawled lifeless in the hallways, no char from explosions or brown splashes of dried blood. This was the place that the-one-who-sees-badly had gone when he walked in the dark one's dream of conquest. He was seeing it without the filter of the *mor'ee-rai*, with his own eyes instead of the eyes of the aliens.

There were many of the Tall Ones here, and many of them dressed in the same way, as if they had no imagination to shape different apparel. They moved purposefully through the halls, as if always in a hurry. Some of them carried the same shapes that the Kayeechi had learned to recognize as weapons, even though they had not seen them used in the dreams. Unfortunately, without the shape of use, they were so many lumps of inert metal to the shapers.

They had the shape they needed, but Etra'ain wanted more. She wanted to understand the relationship between the lifting-machine and the giant egg and the big explosion—was it a Narrai egg? The Kayeechi had spent many hours debating this possibility. Perhaps this had not been a weapon for them to use at all, but instead one that the Narrai would use against them.

When the Tall One leader had called in his dreams, Vair had been delighted to hear and to answer. If this was the place of the secrets of the Tall Ones, he was where he needed to be. And the fact that the Tall Ones were obviously at war with *someone* spoke well for the prospect of finding new shapes.

The realization lent a certain thrill to his explorations, and at the same time provided a map, more or less, of the Complex for him to follow. Instead of wandering randomly through the halls, he decided to head directly for the place the Daniel Tall One called the Gate room. There had been many weapons used there in the dream; perhaps some of them would be there now, available for a curious Kayeechi to examine and shape. Taking such power home would be a triumph indeed, and the Narrai would suffer for it—not for long perhaps, but nothing was perfect, was it? And it would not matter if the flying ones could lay death eggs. Dead Narrai laid no eggs at all.

CHAPTER SIXTEEN

Despite being excluded from the return trip, Jackson and Teal'C opted to observe the "practice run" preparations along with Carter in the infirmary. The three of them made quite an audience as O'Neill lay, still fully clothed, on the bed before them.

"Sweet dreams?" Jackson cracked as he came in.

O'Neill glared at him. Carter hid a smile, not very successfully; it was something she would have liked to say, but when it came right down to it, Jack O'Neill was still her superior officer.

"I doubt it," Teal'C weighed in. "Even without the incense burning all around, some residual effects may remain." It wasn't that Teal'C had no sense of humor—far from it—but he was the most grimly pragmatic of the four of them.

"I ran some blood tests, but a full tox scan

takes more time," Frasier said. "But what you say is certainly possible. Colonel?"

Feeling a little self-conscious in his lying-in-state position, O'Neill sat up and swung his legs over the edge of the bed in one smooth movement. His toes curled inside his socks at the chill of the industrial-grade linoleum of the infirmary floor. The military had its own odd ideas about interior decorating. "I had some dreams," he admitted. "Nothing bad, really. No real disasters, no weapons tests."

"That's a relief," Jackson said. "Did you know you were dreaming?" All attempts at levity had vanished, and his blue eyes were serious behind the wire-framed glasses.

"Uh, no. At least I don't think so. I can't remember it very well," O'Neill admitted, running his hands through his hair and cracking a huge yawn. "I feel better though if that makes any difference."

"Being aware that you're dreaming usually means you wake up," Janet said as the other members of the team arranged themselves in chairs around the bed. "It's a very, very fine line to walk. I think I can use this technique to help you maintain that line. But General Hammond's right. We want to make sure before we try it under field conditions."

"Whatever the heck those are in this case,"

O'Neill said, yawning again. "Okay, Doc. Teach me how to lucid dream and we're outta here."

Frasier laughed. "It's not quite that easy. Normally, researchers look for people who dream vividly—"

"*Not* a problem here," Jackson interjected.

"And who remember their dreams in detail when they wake up," the doctor went on, ignoring the interruption. "Since we don't have the luxury of conditioning the colonel over time, we're going to take the direct approach." She pulled out a black box with wires hanging in all directions and set it on a nearby instrument cart, plugging the unit into a wall outlet. A series of lights, dials, numbers, graphs, light-emitting diodes, and other readouts hummed into life. She maneuvered the cart beside the bed until she was satisfied with its placement.

"Uh, is that what I think it is?" O'Neill straightened in alarm.

"That depends on what you think it is, Colonel. If you don't already know, it would take roughly a couple of hours to explain it. What it does— what I'm going to do—is stimulate the dream centers of your brain, reproducing the level of electrical activity characteristic of the lucid-dreaming state and hope that you can take the cue."

"We're not talking actual cutting-in-the-head brain surgery are we?"

"Well," she said thoughtfully, "that would probably make for much more precise control. But I don't think the General would let me try. And there's all that fuss about human experimentation. So no brain surgery. Nothing invasive. There should be no side effects at all. You're just going to fall asleep." She sounded mildly regretful at the prospect.

"You think I'm going to 'just fall asleep' with everybody staring at me like this?" the colonel groused, indicating his fascinated audience. She pushed him back into a reclining position on the bed. After some automatic resistance, he swung his feet back up again and forced himself to relax. The others shifted position to get a clearer view. O'Neill made a face at them.

"Oh, yes." She smiled down at him, brushing a military-short lock of hair out of the way of a sticky patch of electrode fixative and freeing up the wire that led from the skin contact patch to the machine parked on the instrument cart. "I'm pretty sure we won't have to shave your head, either. Much." She intoned in a sepulchral voice. "You are about to embark on a voyage of danger and discovery to the innermost depths of the imagination."

O'Neill looked at her as if she had lost her mind.

"Sorry. I've always wanted to say something like that," she apologized without a trace of remorse, continuing to place the contacts. "I'm an old *Twilight Zone* addict."

"There's a lot you haven't told us, isn't there, Doctor?" O'Neill groused.

"Don't worry. I used to date a neuropathologist in med school," she said cheerfully. "I think I remember how to do this." The electrodes were attached to the black metal box, and the readouts began to flicker wildly. She checked the readings and then sat on the bed beside him, addressing the rest of the team as well as O'Neill.

"Before I came into the debriefing, I did some quick research to refresh my memory on the important points," she said. "Getting the colonel to sleep isn't going to be the problem. Getting him through the various stages of sleep into the REM state, where he's dreaming, isn't going to be difficult either. The problem is that the human mind tends to seek safety from its dreams by waking up. We need dreams for reasons we don't understand, but once we realize that we're dreaming, the mind shuts down the dream and we regain consciousness."

"And a good thing too," Carter remarked.

"Usually it's just before you hit the ground or something."

"There are several stages of sleep. The first stage when you're just dozing, we call alpha. The second, beta, is REM sleep, when you dream. That's the one we want. Humans have to get REM sleep in order to get any rest. Then there are deeper stages, some of which almost approximate complete unconsciousness. Not everyone experiences those."

"You sounded a lot more sure of yourself when you were talking to Hammond," O'Neill said suspiciously. The contact cream for the electrodes itched, and he lifted his hand to scratch at one and then changed his mind, deciding to suffer manfully instead.

Frasier gave him an approving, if absentminded, smile; she was focused on his comment. "The theory is sound. It's even been tested. But every subject is different. The more strong-willed they are, the more they have to work to let themselves continue dreaming."

"I realized I was dreaming on P4V-837," Carter said. "But I didn't wake up. The dream just kept going on and on."

"Same here," Jackson said.

"And I," Teal'C confirmed. "I attempted to awaken and could not. Does that imply we are weak of will?"

"No, but you said that the aliens interacted with you in the dreams. So they may have used their abilities to keep you in that state. Your problem," she was addressing O'Neill directly now, "will then be *not* letting them know you know what they're doing and not letting them prevent you from carrying out the mission."

"And how exactly am I supposed to keep myself from waking up once I figure I'm dreaming?" he asked, wiggling the skin of his forehead against the itch of the adhesive. "And if I do stay asleep, how do I make the dream go the way I want it to? I couldn't do that before. I just kept trying things that didn't work, but none of them were really my idea."

"It sounds as if on P4V-837 the natives were providing the stimulation to get the response they were looking for. What we're going to do now is beat them to the punch and provide our own stimulation."

She reached for the controls on the box. "I'm not going to bother trying to hypnotize you or give you suggestions. Let's just see where it takes you. I'll only run this for a couple of minutes. Two minutes exactly, in fact." She checked her watch.

"I hope that thing's battery power—" The sentence was interrupted. O'Neill's jaw slackened. His eyes were closed.

"Is he asleep?" Carter whispered. "Already?"

"Oh, you don't have to whisper," Frasier said in a normal voice. The others flinched, looking at the unchanged relaxation on O'Neill's face. "He's not going to have a problem staying asleep. In fact, he isn't going to be *able* to wake up until the impulses stop. What I'm trying to do now is bring him into a beta state where he can dream and—we hope—realize he's dreaming." She touched the controls delicately.

Field of butterflies. Bright sunshine, warm, just a little breeze, enough to keep the brightly colored monarchs in the air, not enough to blow them away. Blue flowers in the field, blue and yellow against the green, green grass. He reached out a hand, and an inquisitive butterfly landed on his fingertips. Bringing the hand closer to his face, slowly, slowly, he studied the gently waving wings, the elegant antennae.

It felt funny somehow. He looked at the butterfly, and the butterfly looked back at him. He felt as if he were pushing up against something, some barrier, but there was no barrier here. There was only himself in a summer field surrounded by butterflies, a soft warm breeze on his face.

And something kept pushing back at him. Holding him down. He could fly or at least float, he thought, if it weren't for whatever it was.

The butterfly was looking back at him. The antennae were growing out of a head marked with lines of short red fur. It clashed horribly with the elegant yellow and blue wings that moved hypnotically back and forth.

Vair winked at him.

He was dreaming.

The jolt of awareness almost woke him up completely, shoving him up against the barrier again. But he was still in the meadow, looking at the butterfly. The fact that he was trapped in the dream, *couldn't* wake up, panicked him, and he fled deeper into unconsciousness.

"Damn," Janet said and tweaked the controls again. "No, don't worry," she reassured the apprehensive team surrounding her. "He's just dropped into a deeper sleep level. I'll bring him back into the beta zone."

He wasn't going to be allowed to rest. The pressure kept bringing him back, back, back. He understood once more that he was dreaming, and he tried to dive back into the comforting, dreamfree darkness without success. Frustrated, he roared at the field of butterflies, and they all fled save the one that was still clinging to his fingertips, no matter how hard he tried to shake it off. Vair yelped in protest, a tiny, tinny voice he could somehow hear clearly above all the noise he himself was making, and it made him angrier.

"Ow!" Carter said as O'Neill's arm hit her across the chest. She moved back and away from the bed and its thrashing occupant.

Wait—there's a reason. There's a mission. Practice.

Once more he brought the butterfly up to his face.

"Okay, little guy, fly away," he said. "Go join your buddies. See, they're waiting for you."

"Did he say something?" Daniel asked.

Frasier shrugged. "Talking in his sleep?"

The butterfly waved its wings back and forth with hypnotic slowness, unimpressed by the patently false croon.

"You're supposed to fly away when I tell you to," O'Neill said, gritting his teeth. "Go on. Go!"

The butterfly remained. Its head did, however, transform from that of a small red-furred alien back into that of a gray, fuzzy, big-eyed bug.

"Well, if I can't control you, I can still control me." With that, O'Neill turned his back on the green field and started to walk away. The butterfly swung helplessly from his fingertips.

He woke up.

He found himself staring into a circle of worried eyes. They were friends, that much he knew immediately. It took him a few moments to adjust to the idea that he really *was* awake, back in the infirmary. His most immediate reaction was irritation. "What did you wake me up for?" he complained querulously. "I was gonna get rid of it. If you just gave me a couple more hours."

The team exchanged glances.

"You had two minutes, exactly as I promise you, Colonel," Janet said. "But time in dreams isn't like time in the waking world. It might have seemed like hours to you."

"Rid of what, Colonel?" Carter asked.

"The butterfly. It wouldn't go away when I told it to, and then you woke me up." He yawned mightily.

"Tell us what happened," Janet said, removing the electrodes. "Did you realize you were dreaming?"

His brow furrowed beneath the clinging electrodes as he tried to grasp the memories, already beginning to fade. "Yeah, sure. That part worked just fine. I just couldn't get the damn flutterby to go away when I told it to. All the others went. There was just this one hanging around. Damn thing looked like Vair."

"That doesn't sound good," Jackson observed.

"If we had been available to help, we could have removed the butterfly, Daniel Jackson."

"Don't you think I can get rid of a damned butterfly by myself, Teal'C?"

"But, sir," Carter interrupted gently. "That's

why we're a team, isn't it? So you don't have to?"

"Yeah, well, dammit, let's try this again, shall we? If this plan is gonna work, I'd better practice a little harder. I'm *not* going to be outsmarted by little fuzzy aliens, dammit."

Meanwhile, one of the little, fuzzy aliens in question was becoming more and more bewildered as he sought the Gate room and, incidentally, something useful from the Tall Ones. At one point he entered a small room, only to have the doors slide shut behind him. When they opened again, it was to reveal a completely new set of hallways and rooms. And it was getting more and more difficult to stay unnoticed. Even when the Tall Ones failed to see him, others noticed the epidemic of rubbed eyes and abruptly shaken heads where he had Shaped past, a fleeting impression that could not be pinned down.

He had come to this place to do reconnaissance on the strange Tall Ones, to see if they were any threat—no, in truth, to steal whatever he could from them in aid of his own people's battles. Steal, because those who were not Kayeechi could not understand the Shaping, the dreamwalk. It made peaceful contact impossible, just as it was impossible with the Narrai.

But this place was a horror. Things without

souls watched on behalf of the Tall Ones, spoke for them, recorded bits and pieces of the fleeting signs of his passage. He did not know this place well enough to shape it true, and despaired of being able to shape it at all.

There were wonders aplenty—suns and nights born from a tiny stick on the wall or a button—yet he had seen no true sun since he'd found himself in this place. It was a vast place; only pieces of it were familiar from the dreaming. These Tall Ones must be very powerful indeed to have made such intricacies. The great light must be but a small part of what they could do to their enemies. If he could only find the place they stored such weapons, such wonders!

He scuttled into yet another of the endless rooms and found himself looking down through a clear wall at a stone circle much like the one at home. At the foot of the circle, the aliens were setting yet another of their machines in place. He could hear a great voice talking: ". . . SIX encoded . . ."

A few heartbeats later, the Gate below him opened with a roar, and he saw that his hands were leaving sweat marks on the clear wall in front of him.

The little machine waited until the Gate had settled itself and then trundled through.

He could remember snatches of dreams about

traveling through a Gate. It was cold. Much, much better to Shape through dreams.

But even though he had found the Gate, there were no new weapons he could use here. He watched the shimmer of the Gate a while longer and then gave up, barely avoiding a pair of Tall Ones who were entering the room as he left it.

One of them looked after him, puzzled, but by that time Vair had Shaped emptiness, and there was nothing to see.

He was getting a little desperate.

The Tall One who had opened the way for him was sleeping again. He slept a great deal, Vair thought, but that was so much the better for him. He could feel the Tall One's mind tugging at him, seeking to draw him out of the Shaping and back into the dream, but Vair had walked in many places, and the Tall One was a child in such things.

And that in itself was confusing. How could they have all these things without Shaping? They must somehow but they didn't. It was more than an honest Kayeechi could understand. His grip tightened on the hilt of his knife as he shaped away from the seeking eyes of more of the aliens.

Vair found himself in a small room with a door that led into yet another room. There were metal boxes and tables everywhere. There were handles set in the sides of some of the boxes; he tugged on one, experimentally, and the side slid out smoothly, becoming a box itself, full of mysterious black things, cords and thin flat discs perfect in their similarity.

A noise came from the inner room, and Vair stepped back behind the taller of the boxes as yet another Tall One stepped out and sat in a chair wedged into a tiny opening.

What is this? Vair demanded, tired of not having names for these shapes.

Desk. Filing cabinet. Drawer. Computer. Disks, came the answers from the sleeping Tall One, and then the answers stopped abruptly, as if something about them had startled the sleeper. He could not ask for too much for fear of waking him; too many demands focused the mind.

Vair shaped past the seated Tall One and its *desk* to go through the inner door and see what he could find.

He was disappointed to discover only another room, larger than the first, with yet another Tall One seated behind a desk examining a *file*. In one corner of the room was a pole from which hung a striped banner, and behind the human was a symbol on the wall. This desk was made of wood, while the one in the outer room was metal, and there were no filing cabinets here. This alien, like many of the others, was dressed in blue cloth with many symbols attached; watching him, Vair tried to shape his tunic to match without much success. He felt a rush of pity for this Tall One. While all the aliens were sadly lacking in facial patterns as far as he could tell, this one, he noted with a shudder of horror, didn't even have a full cranial cap as the others did. He wondered what evil fate had befallen this unfortunate and how he still lived despite it all.

It seemed oblivious to its deformation. It sighed in exasperation and turned a *page*. It was, the sleeper informed him when he coaxed once again, *reading*. Vair could not understand what might be so fascinating about the thin leaves with symbols on them.

Still, what interested a Tall One might be useful, so he came around the desk and looked over its shoulder.

His cheek brushed lightly against a hairless pate, and the Tall One jerked around in irritation at the tickling.

Which was how George Hammond found himself nose to nose, finally and unmistakably, with a Kayeechi.

CHAPTER SEVENTEEN

The roar the general let out was enough to frighten almost anyone, let alone the sergeant sitting in the front office. Vair, who had faced angry Narrai over their own nests with the splattered yolk of their eggs oozing between his toes, was nearly as startled, but only by the fact that the Tall One's reaction had included a direct grab for his throat. The horribly multiple fingers managed to close only on a wisp of his fur before he Shaped himself away. He did not linger for the invasion of summoned security.

"Sir, are you sure—"

It wasn't a wise question to ask a general. He was emphatically sure, and it was up to the major in charge of the day watch to find the intruder.

That wisp was evidence enough, as far as George Hammond was concerned. Once the scientists got hold of it, they agreed that it was indisputably not of this Earth. However, that left unanswered the question of how the alien had penetrated the Complex—even unto the CO's sanctum sanctorum—and where it was now. Surveillance tapes were pulled and reviewed. Security personnel were questioned closely. And SG-1 was summoned forthwith out of the infirmary and to the general's office.

"What do you know about this, people?" he asked.

"Nothing, sir," they responded.

"Honest," O'Neill added plaintively.

"What did it look like, sir?" Jackson inquired earnestly.

Hammond glared, aware that his next words would in any rational world brand him as a hopeless crackpot. Fortunately things at the Stargate Complex were not always entirely rational. "I saw a little fellow, not very tall. He was wearing an Air Force uniform. He had big blue eyes and a funny pattern of hair outlining his eyes and mouth and . . . I think it was his nose. I grabbed for him and got hold of a scrap of the hair," he added, not quite defensively.

Rather than questioning his sanity, the team looked at O'Neill, who said in a strangled voice, "Sir? What color was the hair?"

"Red. Sort of auburnish. Why?"

"I think I know who it was."

The team looked startled. Its leader looked ill. "I think it was Vair," he continued as if he was reluctant to reach his conclusion. "He showed up in my dream. Dr. Frasier and I were trying out this lucid-dreaming thing, and he was there.

"And it looks like now he's *here*. Somewhere."

"Are you telling me," Hammond said grimly, "that this was just something you . . . dreamed up? This thing got through our security as if it didn't exist, because you were *dreaming* about it?"

"Uh," O'Neill responded, uncharacteristically groping for words. "Well, sir, I don't know how else it could have happened." He, along with the others, was standing at rigid attention in front of Hammond's desk. Even Jackson, who had the military background of a tree sloth, was exhibiting his very best posture.

"Oh, at ease," Hammond snarled. Jackson slumped. Carter and O'Neill assumed a position of parade rest and waited for the next onslaught. Teal'C shifted his weight slightly.

"Look at these tapes," Hammond said, punching up a series of vidcaps on the wall monitor behind his desk. "Tell me what you see."

"Vair," O'Neill said promptly. "That's him. Absolutely."

The others agreed.

"But where'd he go?" Carter asked a moment later. The space on the tape that had been occupied by a small alien was now occupied by an empty corridor.

"Now you see him, now you don't," Jackson murmured.

"Dr. Jackson, your report assures me that these aliens possess a very primitive technology. And aside from their talent for teleportation and psychokinesis and pulling things wholesale out of people's heads, I suppose you may be right." Hammond's words were laced with heavy sarcasm.

"I do *not*, however, welcome the idea that they may traipse through this facility at will just because someone has a bad dream! I want this stopped, Colonel. I want this hole plugged. Am I making myself clear about this?"

"Yes sir," O'Neill said, because that was what one said to a general in this kind of mood.

"And I want this Vair, or whatever his name is, captured!"

"Easier said than done," Jackson murmured. The rest of them stared straight ahead, not daring to look at their civilian colleague.

"What exactly do you mean by that, Dr. Jackson?"

Jackson swallowed. "Well, sir, he might not actually *be* here, if you see what I mean."

"I do not," Hammond barked. His fingertips rolled against each other as if seeking a sensation that had been experienced and was now gone. "I saw him. I pulled some of his hair. They're looking at it in the lab right now. What do you mean, he might not be here?"

"Well, sir—" Jackson looked at the others, but they could offer no help. "I think maybe Vair's being here is, well, part of the Shaping that the Kayeechi do. It's not actually clear where their reality really lies.

"He could be here as a result of Jack's dream, but in the long run I don't think he's really *here* here."

"And how do you explain the hair, Dr. Jackson?"

"Well, sir . . ." Jackson took a deep breath. "Maybe it was part of his created reality."

"Dr. Jackson, you are making absolutely no sense at all. I have concrete evidence of the physical reality of that alien in my office. He was here. That means he's still here in this Complex, and I want him found."

"Unless he's gone back home the same way he came, sir."

Hammond opened his mouth to blast the younger man into oblivion, then closed it again slowly. "If that's the case, Doctor, how can we ensure our security? We've got no way to con-

trol or deny him access or even keep him once
we've caught him."

Jackson had no answer for that one.

"That's security's worst nightmare," Carter
remarked. Then she looked as if she wished she
hadn't. The words fell into a little pool of silence. No one had the courage to comment on
the inadvertant pun.

"Sir—" O'Neill dared to push his luck.

"Yes, Colonel?"

O'Neill had a feeling that he'd better come up
with something good or that might be the last
time he was addressed by that particular rank.

"Sir, given that there seems to be a link between the alien Vair and myself, there's no reason to assume that a similar link doesn't exist
between the other members of the team and the
other Kayeechi who were in their dreams. Although," he added with painful honesty, "Vair
was the main one."

"So if the rest of you fall asleep, you may
open the way for a whole horde of these beings?
Let me guess. You think you should all go back
on this wild-goose chase," the general growled.
"What are you going to do when you get there?
Ask them pretty please not to do this anymore?
I don't think lucid dreaming is the solution."

"Sir, we don't know what the solution is. All
we know is there seems to be a link between

us—me anyway—and one of the Kayeechi. I can't break that link here. It doesn't matter anymore if I'm awake or not. He seems to have full access to the place. We have to assume that all the others—Eleb, Etra'ain, Shasee, who knows how many others—will too. Unless we all go back, I don't know how we can close all the doors." He paused. "I'm not sure how we can anyway, but I *am* sure we can't find the solution on Earth."

Hammond stared at him. "You understand, don't you, Colonel, that unless those doors can be closed, you and your team are a threat to the security of this planet? As you've just pointed out, we have no way of knowing what else might materialize through your dreams."

O'Neill swallowed, imagining a roc let loose in the Gate room. "Yes, sir."

"I would hate to lose this team, Colonel. But I'm prepared to if necessary. The four of you—and Dr. Frasier—are ordered to return to P4V-837 to resolve this issue—and you may not come back until you have."

"Yes, sir."

A thorough search of the Complex and an intensive review of surveillance tapes revealed no signs of the alien once it had disappeared from Hammond's office. Nonetheless, SGC Security made it a point to continue the search through the night. Meanwhile, SG-1 forced itself to get a few hours sleep before trying to complete their preparations to go through the Gate once more.

The next morning, Frasier coached O'Neill on various exercises related to dreaming while the others reviewed their gear and prepared for possible permanent exile.

"Can you remember some of the characteristics of your usual dreams, Colonel?" she asked him as they sat in her office. He, at least, was rested. She was given to looking over her shoulder and jumping at shadows.

"Um." He looked at her, his lips twitching. "Not that I'm inclined to share."

She blushed a little. "I mean, can you recall something from a dream that struck you as so bizarre that it could only *be* a dream? It doesn't have to be anything big. Some people report being in places they haven't been for years, or—"

"Coming to work naked?" he asked helpfully.

"That's a common one." She refused to let him fluster her. She was the doctor, dammit. "What I'm looking for is something that you can use to tell yourself you're in a dream state. It could be anything: a cartoon watch or dress gloves that are the wrong color. We can't practice here anymore, so it might help to decide ahead of time, if you can, on something to use as a personal cue. With the watch, for example, you could will it to change to a different kind. From Mickey Mouse to a diver's watch, for instance."

"But I *like* my Mickey Mouse watch," he said gravely.

It was just her luck to have to deal with a bird colonel with a warped sense of humor. She gritted her teeth and went on. "Then change something else. Do you want to review reports of failed tests to get some ideas of how you can sabotage the Kayeechi's potential bomb?"

"There's that too, isn't there?" he said thoughtfully. "I wonder if they wipe themselves out on their own world if they'll just dream their way into ours."

"Hammond would have our hides for rugs."

He let his breath go. "Yeah, I think he would. Okay. Watches. Gloves. Bombs. Anything else we need?"

"Nose filters." She began roaming around her office, stacking items on the desk between them. "The stimulator. Food?"

"Logistics will take care of that. Concentrates and water purifiers," he told her. "How good are these filters of yours?"

"You could walk through a field of angry skunks and never notice," she assured him and set several packs of the filters on the growing pile. "I think I want to take my own first-aid kit."

"Good plan."

"Look, Colonel, you do this all the time. I don't. If you can be helpful, that's fine, but—"

"Hey, hey, hey. It's okay, Janet." He was on his feet and next to her, not quite touching her. "Look, there's no reason why you have to go. Show Carter how to work the stimulator. We might have to be trapped there, but you don't."

She looked up at him, touched by the concern in his dark eyes. "I'm not afraid of the assignment, Colonel. And I can't teach Carter how to operate this well enough to be sure she might not accidentally burn your brain out. I have to go. It's my job, just like it's your job."

He hesitated, then seemed to realize how close he was standing to her and stepped back, creating more room between them. "All right," he said at last. "How about I get out of your way and look for some of those reports you mentioned. We'll meet in the Gate room in three hours."

"That will be fine, Colonel." She watched him leave the office and told herself it was a good thing he wasn't underfoot while she was trying to pack. It wasn't quite convincing, even to herself.

* * *

The Council of the Kayeechi—Those Who Shape—huddled under the feast canopy, ignoring the thin wails from their prisoner. It was raining, a steady drumbeat of heavy drops, and the thatch of the canopy did only an adequate job of sheltering them. Every so often the weight of water on a low place in the covering overcame the woven vegetation, and a small splash and the annoyed exclamation of a Councillor indicated that there was yet another hole.

There was no energy left in them to Shape the canopy's integrity. The eight of them moved out of the way of the leaks and stared at each other, waiting.

They were waiting none too patiently for Vair.

"I still think," Shasee said with an air of having repeated herself too many times, "we should try to *talk* to them. It was a mistake, after all."

Eleb snorted, but it was Etra'ain who remarked acidly, "There was no mistake. We were eager for the feasting, all of us. If I remember aright, you were among the first to praise Vair's courage and cunning when he came back that first time."

"But we didn't know they were *people*," Shasee protested. "If we had known—"

"Vair knew. He could not have watched them so long in order to find a nest unguarded without knowing. And when he came back, his patterns still sticky with yolk, telling the heroic tale of battling Narrai from the middle of their own nest"—Etra'ain's voice was especially sarcastic now—"you sang his praises."

"So did you," Shasee whispered. "Everyone did."

"I was hungry. We were all hungry. We were starving. And he had come back with the biggest egg any of us had ever seen."

There was another anguished wail from the cage. A claw came out, waving helplessly, and knocked aside some of the more useless debris from the last Shaping. The Council ignored it.

"That egg was already going bad anyway," Eleb muttered. "It wasn't *that* good."

"The next one was," someone else piped up. "I liked it."

"So where is our intrepid hero now?" Etra'ain snarled. "These Earth people will be another Narrai, I think."

"At least we haven't eaten any of them yet," Eleb pointed out.

"They had strong dreams," Shasee, ever the optimist, said. "Very strong. There was great power."

Etra'ain shook raindrops out of her hair. "Which we could not walk in long enough to use. Useless! *Where* is Vair?"

"Here," said Vair. His red fur was dry, except

where the canopy drips had caught him and, in one place, where the regular patterns and lines had been interrupted by a patch of naked blood. Shasee and others murmured in shock and sympathy. Vair pretended to ignore them. "And I have good news. We have another chance. They're worried about us. They're coming back. And this time I can control the Tall One. I have walked in his mind and stepped outside it. Even you have not done such a thing, Etra'ain."

Etra'ain snorted. "You have no idea what I have done or can do, Vair. As for controlling the Tall One's dreams—show us and we will believe you."

"All right," Vair responded defiantly. "I will."

No matter how many times you heard about it or even experienced it, Janet Frasier thought, going through the Stargate had to be a shock to the system. As she stumbled out the other end, only to be caught and held up—and placed gently back on her feet—by Teal'C, she made a mental note to do more studies on the cumulative effect of wormhole travel. At some point, surely, the human body had to give up on this freezing-thawing cycle?

Frasier herself, as well as all the members of SG-l, wore discreet nose filters guaranteed to block anything larger than a microvirus. They should certainly be effective against pollen and smoke, she'd assured the team. Daniel Jackson was pinching at his nose as if expecting to sneeze, but the sneeze never came. She looked around, fascinated, and was surprised to see the team doing exactly the same thing.

"What's the matter?" she asked, once her teeth stopped chattering.

"That was where we saw the trees moving," Carter informed her. "It didn't look anything like this the first time." The major pointed to a mountain that rose up less than half a mile away, evidently the product of a massive geologic fault slip. "That mountain wasn't there. And it looks like they've had a bad fire season in the last forty-eight hours." The slope rising to the foothills was blackened in places, and the few stubby trees were charred and bare.

"The roc was over there," Jackson added, looking a few degrees off the direction of the mountains. "Came in from that direction to grapple with a tree." He paused. "We must have been in someone else's dream at the time and not even realized it. Just stepped out of the Gate and right into the middle of it."

That's impossible, Janet thought, but wisely kept her mouth shut.

"There are smudge pots set around the Gate,"

Teal'C noted. "They appear similar to the ones used in the eating areas."

"I wonder if that's what I thought was the smell of flowers blooming the last time," O'Neill remarked, pivoting in place to scan the horizon. At least the DHD was still there. "Or if maybe they're hoping we'd be back."

"Or *someone* would be back anyway." Daniel was peering up into the sky, shielding his eyes from the sun, apparently trying to identify something that was ducking through a collection of white puffy clouds.

Frasier nodded. From the descriptions the team had given her, she'd expected this world to be a pleasant place. And it was, if you discounted the evidence of repeated forest and grass fires and the flying creatures circling above like vultures on her own planet. Sunny, warm—just like home. Even the burned-out area reminded her of home—Montana, say.

"The village, or whatever it was, was over there," O'Neill said. "Since the welcoming committee is somewhere else at the moment, let's go see what the place *really* looks like."

"And keep your eyes peeled for bombs while we're at it," Jackson joked.

"Yeah, do that," O'Neill echoed. He wasn't joking at all.

They made their way through a burned-out

patch of trees along the base of the cliffs, the raw charcoaled stumps sticking pointed fingers up into the sky. Beneath their feet dead vegetation crunched.

"What's that?" Frasier asked at one point.

The team paused to look up at a bundle hanging from the remains of a branch. "I think that's the enemy," O'Neill said. "Or what's left of one."

"We're not getting radiation readings, are we?" Carter asked, trying to keep a note of practicality in her voice.

"Not yet," Jackson replied, examining a Geiger counter. It ticked softly, irregularly. "All I get is low counts, probably background radiation. So far, so good."

"The Kayeechi approach," Teal'C announced, speaking for the first time.

"Oh, how *cute!*" Frasier exclaimed. Diminutive and quick moving, they chattered to each other as they came closer, and her attention was caught by the various patterns and colors of hair on their visible skin.

Then she noticed what the cute little furry aliens were carrying in their three-fingered hands: Jaffa energy staffs, half size, and a few automatic rifles and sidearms, similarly downsized. "Uh, well—"

"That's okay. General Hammond would have

thought they were cute too," Carter said in a low voice, "if Vair hadn't sneaked up on him."

The team stopped and waited, weapons ready, for Etra'ain and her escort to come to them. The two groups regarded each other warily.

"There's Vair and Shasee," Jackson informed Frasier. "The red and the gray ones. They were the ones we met first."

"Vair? I thought you said Vair was—"

"I did," O'Neill said grimly. "And no, I don't know how he got back here. Or if he's still back *there* too. I plan to find out."

"Why have you returned?" Etra'ain called out. Her voice was thin across the intervening distance.

"Major, why don't you tell them?" O'Neill said out of the corner of his mouth. "It isn't *my* eyeliner."

"Ritual religious object," Carter corrected and moved a few feet toward the aliens. The rest of the team grouped itself behind her. She spread her hands in front of her body, showing them empty. The Kayeechi muttered. Behind her she could hear Jackson identifying the purple-furred one as the probable leader of the aliens.

"We have returned to recover an object we inadvertently left behind," she said. "We've come a very long way. We know that there was anger between us when we left. We ask that you allow us to return to the cave where we slept to search for my . . . object."

Out of the corner of her eye, she could see O'Neill making a production out of a yawn, stretching, doing his best to look like a man in need of a nap. "We don't want to cause trouble," she said. "Let us find this thing, and we will go peacefully on our way."

The aliens huddled. They appeared to be arguing passionately, if the amount of gesticulation involved were any indication. Vair, she noted with interest, hung back from the discussion, staring at O'Neill and the rest of them. The other Kayeechi seemed to find this behavior uncharacteristic of him, judging by the looks they gave him as they argued. She was willing to bet that Vair hadn't told anyone about his visit to the Complex—always assuming, of course, that this was the same Vair.

At last Etra'ain stepped out of the colorful group and approached Carter. "You are weary," she said. "We understand that you are strangers and do not know our ways. We asked you for help, but perhaps we were importunate. Come and let us give you food and rest. Let us help you search. Be our guests once again."

"You are very kind," the major responded. Glancing at the armed escort, she added, "Could you ask them to point those things somewhere else? Straight up maybe?"

Etra'ain looked from Carter to Teal'C to her own people and then went back to engage in a hasty discussion. The result of this was that the energy staffs carried by her escort were vertical, though some were barrel end up and others barrel end down.

Either way, they weren't pointed at SG-1. When the aliens moved into two groups, opening a path between them, and Etra'ain gestured, Carter said, "I guess that's our cue, sir."

They followed the aliens to a small clearing, where they paused as Vair, Shasee, Etra'ain, and the others stopped to sort themselves out. "This looks—to me anyway—like where we were before," Jackson remarked. "The trees and park, I mean. Except there's no city."

There was indeed no city. Instead, they saw only a rough huddle of hide-and-thatch huts grouped in an irregular circle around a rectangular area shaded by a hide cover. Here, at least, there were no signs of wildfire. The vegetation looked yellowish, but that might be the bloom of health on this planet.

In the shaded area, the Kayeechi sat and talked to one another, worked industriously on hand weaving, or ate something yellow from shallow straw bowls. At one end of the shaded space, a pen made of stout saplings woven together with vines contained . . . something. A clawed limb occasionally poked through the bars, waved helplessly, and withdrew again. It seemed unable to grasp the bars.

"This has to be where we had the feast," O'Neill said. "I don't remember the cage though. Did any of you see it?"

The rest shook their heads. O'Neill had to force himself to look away from the bars. Those claws looked too much like a human hand might, grasping helplessly at something, anything that might be freedom. A chill of memory ran up his spine, and he shook himself. That claw was *not* a hand, most especially not *his* hand, and for all he knew, the thing might be nothing more than a giant pet canary. Or the cage could be the Kayeechi version of a hospital ward. Or—

"Uh-oh," Carter remarked. "It looks like we're in for round two of the ceremonial greetings."

"Let's see if we can skip the formalities this time." O'Neill greeted the diversion with a sense of relief and forced himself to stop looking at the cage.

But the Kayeechi would not forgo the opportunity to make much of their guests. Once again, platters of food were brought out and spread under the shade of the primitive tarp. Etra'ain stood to welcome them in a short speech that failed to mention there had ever been a battle.

"Doctor, you and Daniel can sit down. Carter, Teal'C and I have religious reasons not to eat tonight," O'Neill said.

Frasier was puzzled for an instant and then understood. She slid the pack off her back with a stifled moan of relief, made sure that her own sidearm was conveniently to hand, and then sat down between two small aliens no taller than seven-year-old girls back home. She noted with relief that Jackson sat on the other side of the alien on her right, and the other three were positioned strategically at her back. All of the miniaturized weapons had been put away; apparently it was rude to eat and shoot. She refused to let that make her feel guilty about having her gun loose in its holster.

One of the large woven platters was set in front of her, and the alien to her right reached for a large red bulb of something and held it out to her.

"Think of it as an apple," Jackson advised. "It was pretty good, as I recall. Of course," he added thoughtfully, turning a similar object over in his hands, "my recall on this world isn't the most trustworthy thing you've ever run into."

"I wish I had one of those instant analyzers they have on science-fiction shows," Frasier fretted, looking at the pots of incense being set unobtrusively around the eating area and the mounds of unidentified fruits and vegetables being presented to them. "I could sure use one right now. It would take me a lab full of equipment to tell what this stuff is."

"Stick around," O'Neill said from behind her with a gallows grin and an undertone. "I'll see if I can dream one up for you." He laughed. "There's an advantage we didn't think of, isn't there?"

"Let's not push our luck," Frasier answered. She managed to take and store samples of nearly everything that was served to them in the steadfast belief that she would be able to analyze them eventually.

"Where's Vair?" Jackson asked the alien between himself and Janet. It had a checkerboard pattern of brown lines, like perpendicular repeating eyebrows, all over its face. "Oh, Dr. Frasier, this is Eleb. We met the last time we were here."

The brown-blocked alien grinned suddenly at her, showing sharp teeth. Frasier had to force herself to treat the grimace as a smile and return it as such.

"Yes, where *is* Vair?" O'Neill repeated. "He was here a few minutes ago, wasn't he?"

Eleb looked confused. "Vair is here. See, he comes."

Sure enough, the red-furred one was making his way through the milling crowd toward them.

"Vair, so good to see you again," O'Neill said. "If we *are* seeing you, that is."

Now it was Vair's turn to look confused, and a three-fingered hand crept up to his cheek, where a raw red patch took the place of a line of fur. "I am here. Where else should I be?"

"We were hoping to discuss that with you," O'Neill said grimly.

"This is not the time for such talk," Etra'ain interrupted. "This is ceremonial. Eat well so that you may sleep well too."

Vair shifted a smudge pot out of the way and sat down beside her, opposite the team, and reached for a handful of soupy grain, apparently relieved at the change of subject.

Frasier looked at the team members. They exchanged bland glances, and Daniel rubbed reflectively at his nose. The doctor hoped that Jackson wasn't going to have a sneezing fit. The filters would never stand up to it.

But the immediate danger, if it was danger, passed, and the archaeologist asked Etra'ain,

"When we left before, we were fighting. Why have you welcomed us back with a feast?"

Carter and O'Neill rolled their eyes—trust Daniel to ask the one question they'd rather not bother with. He, of course, was hot on the trail of an apparently aberrant cultural norm and leaned forward intently for the answer.

Etra'ain's purple three-tiered eyebrows arched high. "We did not wish you to go. Now you have come back. Of course we welcome you. How else should it be?"

The other Kayeechi around her looked at each other as if to say, *It's obvious. Isn't it?*

"You do realize we're going to leave again," O'Neill said dryly.

"That will be when that will be," she said, waving a hand gracefully.

"*Que sera sera*," Carter muttered, forestalling O'Neill, who had opened his mouth to make exactly the same remark.

"That's really interesting," Daniel said, reaching for another piece of bread. "Do you welcome all your enemies that way?"

Etra'ain looked startled and then profoundly offended. "You are not our enemies! We would never share food with enemies. That *thing*"—she indicated the cage—"is our enemy. Not you."

"I see," Daniel said in a tone that indicated he didn't see at all.

"You're in the habit of fighting with your friends then?" O'Neill inquired acidly.

Once again, Etra'ain was startled and then indignant. "Never with our friends." Then she paused as a sudden thought hit her. "Do you have no *leesee* in your world?"

The five from Earth looked at one another. "I guess not," Daniel said. "We don't know what that is."

"*Leesee*. Neither enemy nor friend. Waiting."

"A-huh." It explained a lot. Maybe.

Vair nodded vigorously.

"So," Carter said to him, "when you came—"

"*Leesee*," he interrupted hastily. "You are not yet our friend or our enemy."

"Really," Jackson murmured, and when Carter tried to ask her question again, he offered her another piece of bread, rhapsodizing about how wonderful it was.

It was late by that time, and Etra'ain courteously suggested that perhaps her guests would care to spend the night and rest before continuing their journey. After some protracted discussion, during which the twilight deepened, the teammates agreed that perhaps spending the night would be a very good idea.

After many smiles and reassurances, the five were finally alone.

"He didn't want Etra'ain to know what he had done," Daniel explained later when they had finally broken away from the feast and been escorted to the cave of dreams. "He didn't want you to ask him about it in front of her."

"And if Etra'ain doesn't know about it, maybe the rest don't either," Carter said. "Our little red guy may have ventured out on his own without authorization."

"That still does not solve the problem," Teal'C pointed out. "He may be able to return. He may still tell the others what he has done and how they may do likewise. And we do not know for certain that he himself is not still in the Complex, even though we have seen him here."

"Thank you, Teal'C." It was a masterful summary and definitely not what O'Neill wanted to hear. "We know what the problem is. I'm entertaining solutions now. Anyone?"

"I think it really is Vair," Carter said. "Here, I mean. I never saw anything that indicated they could be in two places at once. Has anyone else?"

The others shook their heads. Frasier, busy setting up her equipment, listened in fascinated silence.

"And he shows the mark where the general pulled out some hair. I think he came back with you, sir. Or he came back anyway."

"I would rather not spend the rest of my life with a little scarlet furry guy following me around, thank you very much," O'Neill said. "How do I get rid of him?"

There was a small silence. No one made any suggestions. From the looks on their faces, Frasier thought SG-1 had all reached the same conclusion, and they didn't like it much.

She couldn't see a way around it either. Evidently, this particular Kayeechi had a way to hook into O'Neill's mind and then step out of it into the surrounding reality. The fact that it hadn't happened with any of the others was not evidence enough that it *wouldn't* or *couldn't* happen sometime in the future—not a comforting thought. And the only way they could be sure O'Neill was going to be permanently rid of Vair was if Vair was gotten rid of. Permanently.

She didn't like that thought, military necessity or not.

"All right," O'Neill said at last, sliding his backpack off his shoulders. "Let's get this show on the road. Janet, you're the boss. Where do you want me?"

She chose to ignore the teasing innuendo and finished the last battery connection. The black box hummed to life, and she twitched a few dials to check its responses.

"You sound like you're not taking this very

seriously all of a sudden," she said, looking up at him from her kneeling position on the dirt floor.

"I'm a doer, not a dreamer." It was a lame joke, and it fell as flat as it deserved to. "I just want to warn all of you, the first person who says, *And then I woke up*, is going to spend a lifetime on KP duty." He sat down beside Frasier. The rest of the team gathered around, seating themselves to watch.

"Well, sir," Frasier said, testing one last connection and untangling one last wire, "I hope you do your dreaming well, because I saw something that looked an awful lot like a WR shell lying beside that cage with the—creature—in it."

Carter sucked in a sudden breath.

" 'WR?' " Jackson asked, pushing his glasses up on his face.

"War Reserve," O'Neill translated grimly. "Weapons components. Why didn't you say something earlier, Janet?"

She shook her head. "It wouldn't have accomplished anything except interrupting the party, and it looked like we had to get through that to get here. Besides, I could have been wrong. I'm not as familiar with those things as I could be."

"Carter or I could have told you whether you

were wrong," he said. For an instant irritation showed in his voice, and then he took a deep breath. "Never mind. It is or it isn't, there isn't anything we can do about it right now. Let's get me hooked up to your machine, Doctor, so you can put me under and we can find some way to deal with this mess."

CHAPTER EIGHTEEN

"Okay," Carter said as O'Neill stretched out on the ground and Janet began attaching electrodes. "Daniel, you're the one who went walking around. I vote we follow you. Wherever the heck it is we're going."

Daniel nodded earnestly. "As soon as Jack's asleep."

As Janet moved to activate the black box, Jack O'Neill caught at her hand. "Aren't you going to wish me sweet dreams?" he asked, the hint of a challenge in his voice.

She looked down at him and the corner of her mouth twitched. "Not this time, Colonel."

"No fun at all, Major." He folded his hands over his chest in pious repose, and she switched the machine on and began monitoring his brain activity.

"Look," Teal'C said suddenly.

The team turned to see Vair standing in the

mouth of the cave, staring at the recumbent figure of Jack O'Neill, his skull now dotted with
black electrode tape. Janet paused, looking to the
team for guidance, unwilling to let the colonel
remain vulnerable if danger threatened.

"Vair. Hello. Greetings," Daniel said, pushing
his glasses up on the bridge of his nose. "What
are you doing here?"

"I have come to offer you *mor'ee-rai*," the little
alien said, staring past Daniel to Frasier and
O'Neill. "You said before that you wished to see
clearly."

"Ah," Daniel said, glancing back at the recumbent colonel. O'Neill, watching the exchange,
closed one eye. "That's . . . that's very kind of you.
Thank you. We certainly do appreciate that."

Vair edged around Daniel, trying to get a better look at the man on the floor, the woman
kneeling beside him, and the strange contraption
he was attached to by black strings. Daniel knew
the little alien could have no idea what the stimulator was or how it was used, but Vair's efforts
still made him uneasy. He interposed himself between the little alien and O'Neill.

"Oh, look," he remarked, in an effort to distract the other. "You've hurt yourself. What happened?"

It got Vair's attention. He looked up at the archaeologist towering over him, and one three-

fingered hand crept up to touch the raw place on his face where a patch of fur had been ripped away.

"It is nothing," he said, edging back from the Tall One in a sudden access of caution. "Nothing. Here . . . here is the *mor'ee-rai*." Producing a small pouch from somewhere within his tunic, he held it out to Daniel. "This will help you see clearly. As you wish to see."

Daniel accepted it, turning it over in his hands to examine the awkward workmanship. It was a badly sewn piece of dark brown leather, discolored in places by the crude tanning process, about the size of the palm of his hand. He could feel the crunch of crumbled vegetable matter sliding around inside it.

"We thank you for your gift," he repeated and shifted closer to Vair as if by accident.

Vair stepped back abruptly. "Place it in the pot and burn it," he said. "I will go now. Sleep well."

"Oh, no doubt," O'Neill remarked with heavy irony as the Kayeechi vanished into the night.

"Well, I guess you've got your sample, Janet," Daniel said. "I wonder what it really is?"

"Most likely not the herb that allows visitors to distinguish reality," Teal'C observed. "It is likely that the Kayeechi expect to plunder our dreams once again."

"Maybe we ought to let one of us use this?"

Daniel opened the pouch and poured a small amount of brownish-gray powder into his hand. "So we know what they expect us to see?"

"Maybe we *need* it to see the colonel's dream," Carter agreed.

"If we use it, how will we know whether we're seeing his dream or not?"

The five of them stared at each other, nonplussed.

"It should not make a difference," Teal'C said slowly, as if testing the idea as he verbalized it. "However the Kayeechi accomplish it, whether through telepathy or some other process, they make dreams real. With the filters, we will see reality. Without them, we will see the dream. But there may not be a difference, if the dream is strong enough. The only way is to try to repeat Daniel's experience. He did actually walk in my dream."

They considered the suggestion.

"That means it's up to you, Jack," Daniel said at last. "Janet, are you sure you can maintain him at a dream level?"

The doctor nodded. "The only problem is whether he has enough practice in realizing that he's dreaming and controlling its direction," she said.

"That's what we're here for," Carter told her with a show of confidence.

No one was fooled.

Janet looked at O'Neill. "Ready, sir?"

"Ready as I'll ever be," he responded, scratching around the drying glue of one electrode. The doctor checked the connections one more time.

"Sweet dreams, sir," she said and turned on the power to the stimulator.

O'Neill struggled for a moment to stay awake. They could see him fighting to keep his eyes open. In only a few moments he lost the battle, his face relaxed, and his breathing slowed and deepened.

Frasier held up one hand. "I want to bring him into the dream state a little more slowly," she said. "Give me a few minutes."

The team stood waiting, self-consciously staring at their leader and each other, and pointedly not looking out the mouth of the cave to see what, if anything, had changed. The indicators on the stimulator glittered and bobbed and finally steadied.

"Okay," she said at last as O'Neill's eyes began darting back and forth under closed eyelids. "We've got ignition. If this is going to work, it should be working now."

"Okay, boss, now what?" Carter asked Jackson. "You were the one who went walkabout before. Lead on."

"Well," he said, suddenly uncertain, "all I did was walk out of the cave." Suiting action to words, he squared his shoulders and stepped outside the rough mouth of their shelter.

The others followed him.

And they found themselves . . . elsewhere.

"What place is this?" Teal'C asked, looking around. It was no longer twilight, but high noon, and the landscape was, if possible, even more desolate than that of P4V-837. They were standing by the side of a one-lane road whose edges were crumbling into the surrounding dirt. The glare of the sun against the pale earth made them squint, and sweat began beading on their foreheads.

"It looks like the Nevada Test Site," Carter said. "I thought we would be with the colonel. What happened?"

"I wasn't with Teal'C when I walked in his dream," Jackson pointed out. "It's not just one person's perspective. It's a whole world. If Jack's dreaming about the Test Site, he's created the whole thing." He looked around with interest. "I've never been here before. Is there *anything* alive out here?"

"There is a scorpion by your foot," Teal'C advised him. Jackson jumped. The pale yellow scorpion curled its tail over its back derisively and skittered away.

"Hey, where's the cave?" Carter asked, turning in a complete circle to take in all of their surroundings. "I thought with these filters we were immune to whatever was in the air. Shouldn't we be able to see the cave?"

There was no cave anywhere in sight, only yellow-white dirt spotted with chamisa and sage as far as the eye could see. Where earth met sky, the two blended together in a featureless haze.

"It's more than just the incense then," Jackson concluded. "They're messing with our minds."

"I *hate* when that happens," Carter grumbled.

"Where should we go then?" Teal'C asked, sticking to the problem at hand. "If this is your test site, then at least we seem to be in the correct dream. If a nuclear test is in process, this is not a good location."

"Good point," Jackson concurred. "*Excellent* point, in fact. Sam, get us outta here. Where would be the most likely place to find Jack?"

"The control point," Carter said. "That's where the observers will be. If he's dreaming about a nuclear test, I'd rather be there than anyplace else anyway. It's in a bunker underground usually."

"Yes, but *where*?" Jackson wanted to know. He kept looking over his shoulder, as if he expected to find a mushroom cloud lurking, ready to jump out at him and say, "Boo!" Or perhaps, "Boom!"

"It could be miles from here," she admitted. "The Test Site is a big place. We need a car of some kind."

"I hear a vehicle," the Jaffa announced. They looked around, but somehow none of them were looking in the right direction when the jeep first appeared, rattling down the crumbling road toward them.

"That's convenient," Carter said wryly.

"It's a *dream*," Jackson pointed out. "These things happen in dreams." As he spoke, the jeep, innocent of either driver or passengers, came to a stop beside them.

"But it's not *our* dream. Is it real?" Carter eyed the car nervously.

Daniel kicked at a tire. It thudded hollowly. "Would you rather walk?"

She decided to concede the point. The three of them got into the car and waited for it to move on.

Nothing happened.

"Why isn't it moving?" Teal'C asked.

"Maybe it figures we know where we're going."

Daniel scanned the bleak horizon. "Riiiiight."

Finally Carter got into the driver's seat and

turned the key. The motor started, and she depressed the clutch and the gas pedal.

"Where are we going?" Daniel said, having relinquished leadership of the expedition to Carter with substantial relief.

"Point Alpha," Carter told him. She set her hands lightly on the wheel and looked around as the jeep started rolling down the crumbling road. "That's where the observation and data recorders are when they did tests."

"Which way is that from here?"

"It's a dream. I'm not sure it matters."

Moments later, she applied the brakes. Before them loomed the mouth of a tunnel, a hole in a giant cliff where moments before there had been no cliff. The road entered the hole. To the right and the left was more desert, bland and unhelpful.

The tunnel looked very much like the entrance to Cheyenne Mountain, but here there were no guards standing by, no barbed wire, only a blank semicircular hole in a sheer granite face.

They got out of the jeep and found themselves standing in a large room filled with people.

Even Carter was taken aback at the abrupt transition. "What the—"

"It's part of the dream," Jackson said. "Jack doesn't like to waste time going places."

Carter looked around nervously. "I wonder

where he and Janet are," she said, unconsciously lowering her voice. "Really are, I mean. This is just too bizarre. I want to pinch myself and wake up."

"Not as much as I did when it happened to me the last time," Jackson said dryly. "Trust me on that one."

They were standing on the top level of four tiers arranged amphitheater-style around a bank of computer screens, next to a flight of steps leading downward that divided each level into two sections. On each successive tier below them were arranged computers, eight on each side of the flight of steps, with outsize monitors and keyboards built into the curving desks.

At each computer sat a short furry figure in a white coat, busily poking at the keyboard with three-fingered hands.

"This is awfully detailed," Jackson said. "Just how involved with nuclear testing *was* Jack anyhow?"

"I don't think he was, but he could have toured the area when he was involved in flight exercises. I did when I was stationed at Nellis. They used to show the place off after the test program was shut down."

"Speak of the devil," Carter remarked. "There he is."

Sure enough, across the room from them, in

front of a bank of monitors, Jack O'Neill was standing, deep in conversation with a group of lab-coated scientists.

"Great," Carter said. "Let's get this show on the road and get back to sanity." The three of them made their way around the half circle of the ampitheater to the colonel. As they approached, one of the diminutive lab-coated "scientists"—none of them were particularly surprised to see that it was Vair—caught sight of them and scurried up to Jack from the other side, earnestly engaging him in conversation. O'Neill bent down to listen to the red-patterned Kayeechi whispering in his ear.

"Uh-oh," Carter observed. "That doesn't look good."

"Jack?" Daniel asked as they came up to the colonel. "Jack, we're here. It's time to get to work."

O'Neill stared at them and, they slowly realized, through them. Daniel's glance fell to Vair, only to see the small alien staring up at them with a smirk.

"You cannot speak to him in the Shaping," Vair said. "He is here with us. You do not belong here. Go away."

"We'd be happy to if you'd just let us take care of one small matter." Daniel reached for the other man's sleeve. "Jack. It's us. Do you know where you are?"

He wasn't sure what he expected. Would the fabric of the sleeve melt and dissipate between his fingers, like so much fog? But it felt real and ordinary and everyday—as real as the dead bodies had looked and smelled when he had walked through the Stargate Complex counting casualties. For all practical purposes it *was* real.

At least the touch of Daniel's hand managed to bring the three others into O'Neill's notice. He shook it off and shot them a confused look.

"Of course I know where I am," he muttered. "Get out of the way. This is important."

Vair was shocked and alarmed by turns as O'Neill responded to the question. He reached for O'Neill's other hand, holding on to it tightly as if to keep the tall man with him.

"Jack, you're dreaming," Daniel persisted. "Remember? Remember the aliens? The lucid dreaming? Janet's monitoring you. You're on P4V-837. Remember?"

"What are you doing?" Vair burst out. "Go away. We need this."

"Got to check the background monitors and seismic sensors," O'Neill said and pushed past them to descend a short series of steps and begin conferring with the Kayeechi. They closed around him almost protectively and began herding him away from the team, and he did not resist.

"He doesn't realize he's dreaming," Carter said with horror. "He thinks this is real, a real test back on Earth."

In the cave, Jack O'Neill mumbled something in his sleep, and Janet looked up sharply at the stimulator readings and fiddled delicately with a knob.

A red-furred hand reached past herself and set itself over hers, twisting sharply.

Jack O'Neill moaned and slumped into himself. Janet jerked around to find herself nose to sharply pointed teeth of a furious red-furred Kayeechi.

Vair snarled at her and pushed her away from the stimulator. She scrambled to her feet and tried to pull him away, but the little alien was surprisingly strong for his size. "What are you doing?" she shouted. "Stop it! You could kill him!"

"You are controlling his Shaping," Vair snarled. "Trying to keep him from doing what we wish him to do. You will stop. It doesn't matter if he dies here. We can keep him in the Shaping, in the dream, long enough to teach us this new weapon." The words came panting through the sharp incisors, puffing against her face as she struggled to push him away.

O'Neill's breathing was too loud, too harsh. She risked a glance at the monitors. He was at the very bottom of the dream cycle, dangerously close to slipping into a coma.

She was a doctor first, sworn to do no harm—but she was a soldier too. On an expedition like this one, she came armed, just as every other team member did. She reached back to unsnap the holster that held her sidearm in place.

Meanwhile, O'Neill was going from one group of diminutive lab-coated scientists to another, looking over their shoulders, pointing to dials and controls. Over their heads, a monitor counted down in large red numerals.

"Oh, no," Carter said. "He's briefing them. He's describing a bomb."

"You've got an inner core and an outer core, and that's surrounded by explosives that push the two cores together into a critical mass," O'Neill was saying.

"We've got to stop him," Carter said. "All these 'scientists' are Kayeechi. They're making notes. We have to shut him up, or they're going to end up knowing everything they need to make a nuclear bomb themselves. Or at least a reasonable facsimile of one."

She trotted across the room and grabbed O'Neill's arm. The scientists to whom he spoke ignored her as if she were invisible. She tried to pull him around to face her, but it was like pulling on a marble monument.

Jackson joined her. "Jack, listen! Please! Remember why you're here! Remember what you're doing! This is a dream! You're in control of the dream!"

This finally got the attention of the rest of the little scientists, who turned to look at the team with expressions of shock on suddenly openly rainbow-furred faces. Jack pushed them away, and Teal'C reached out to take hold of his shoulder.

Unlike Carter's, Teal'C's grip could not be ignored. O'Neill twisted around, his face furious. "What do you think you're doing?" he demanded. "We've got work to do here! You're not cleared to be here!"

As he spoke, doors all around the control area opened, and armed security guards began to pour in.

"That tears it," Carter said and pulled out her automatic. As the security guards moved in on them, she fired a full clip at the control panels.

They blurred, then reappeared, undamaged.

"It's his dream," Jackson said. "He's not going to let us stop him."

"Then we will stop him anyway," Teal'C said and took a zat gun out of the hand of the nearest security guard and carefully shot Jack O'Neill down.

The dream wavered, stuttered. The O'Neill on the floor moaned.

Then the dream solidified again, and instead of being in the control room they were at the bottom of a primitive test tower, with the Kayeechi, still in the miniature lab coats, all gathered around in an earnest audience, taking notes. Next to them was the monitor, counting down the seconds to detonation. "Of *course*," Jackson muttered ironically.

"The wiring," Carter said under her breath as she faced the crowd. "Yank the wiring."

"*Which* wire?"

"Who cares?"

Without hesitation, Teal'C swung himself up to the interlaced girders and began to climb the tower, while Carter raised her hands to catch the attention of the Kayeechi.

"The colonel told you about the cores," she said loudly. The aliens glanced at each other and then at her. "But he didn't finish. You have to remember the cores have to be *purple*. If they're not purple, it won't work. And soak them in prune juice heated to minus forty-three degrees Celsius, and dried in lavender—"

The aliens looked from the crumpled O'Neill to Carter and then to each other as the countdown continued.

"You mean he didn't use prune juice?" she shouted. "It's got to be prune juice! It doesn't work if it's not prune juice, double distilled!"

The aliens continued taking notes.

The countdown reached minus five.

Jackson stepped back and was in the control room again, stepping over O'Neill's body. He hesitated, and then ran to the remaining control panels, frantically flipping switches.

"And when it detonates you get the biggest damn mess you ever saw," Carter went on. "Everybody dies, you hear? *Everybody*. Starting with you because you're right here!"

Teal'C had reached the top of the tower.

In the cave, Janet had pulled her sidearm free.

"And you know what you die of?" Carter went on, suddenly inspired. "They're creatures from Earth and you're allergic to them—horribly allergic—you won't be able to breathe—"

From somewhere invisible and close by, a gunshot cracked.

Teal'C yanked a random wire.

The dream vanished.

In the blink of an eye, they found themselves back in the cave, with a frantic Janet shoving away the dead body of a little, red-furred alien and trying to revive a deeply unconscious O'Neill.

"So it worked?" O'Neill asked groggily, some time later in the "condition serious but not dying" ward at the Complex. "You're sure?"

"We've had a probe monitoring the place," Jackson said. He was back in workout clothes, looking supremely comfortable. "No explosions. Not nuclear anyway."

O'Neill blinked. "And what does that mean, pray tell?"

Daniel snickered and gestured to the other two. Carter blushed and looked down.

"Since the only knowledge the Kayeechi have of nuclear weapons comes from what they were told by us," Teal'C said, "they expect the bright flash and high winds. However, we also informed them that the expected results of the explosion would turn them all into butterflies."

"Butterflies?" O'Neill mumbled, bewildered.

"Yes, butterflies," Carter said finally, grinning. "Let them figure out *that* dream for a change."

"Once upon a time," said the philosopher Chuang Tzu, "I dreamt I was a butterfly.

"I was conscious only of my fancies as a butterfly, and unconscious of my individuality as a man. Suddenly I awoke, and was myself again. Now I do not know whether I was then a man dreaming I was a butterfly, or whether I am now a butterfly dreaming that I am a man."

—Chuang Tzu, ca. 4th C. B.C.

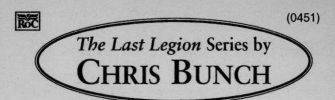